The Chronicles of Origin

Rise of Ares
Part 1

Aron Taylor

WIZARD'S KEEP PUBLISHING

The Chronicles of Origin : Rise of Ares Part 1
Copyright © 2016 Aron Taylor

This book is a work of fiction. Names, characters, businesses, organiza- tions, places, events and incidents either are the product of the author's imagination or are used fictitiously. Any resemblance to actual persons, living or dead, events, or locales is entirely coincidental.

For information contact :
Wizard's Keep Publishing
http://www.wizardskeeppublishing.com
email: info@wizardskeeppublishing.com

ISBN: 978-1-945737-05-3(paperback)
        978-1-945737-06-0(hardcover)
        978-1-945737-07-7(ebook)

LCCN: 2016957028

Cover Design by Josh Tam
http://joshtam.net

First Edition: October 2016

10 9 8 7 6 5 4 3 2 1

Dedicated to My Son
Michael

\

Castaway

"For Ares, lord of strife, Who doth the swaying scales of battle hold, War's money-changer, giving dust for gold, Sends back, to hearts that held them dear, Scant ash of warriors, wept with many a tear, Light to the hand, but heavy to the soul; Yea, fills the light urn full, With what survived the flame—Death's dusty measure of a hero's frame!"

-Aeschylus, Agamemnon

It had been days since he had anything to eat or drink. The darkness of the box was disorienting. How had this happened? How had everything come to this point? Leaning against the smooth cold surface, Michael thought about everything that had happened. Why him? Why was he destined to suffer, to see his friends, family, those he cared for maimed at the hands of savages while God's, those beings with unlimited power, watched and did nothing?

Alone for the last time, Michael screamed in the agony of his soul, "Why are you doing this to me?" Not speaking to his captors, not speaking to himself, he was addressing the Old

Man "Great Spirit" who had sent him into further destruction.

The most difficult thing about being held captive is the helplessness. The forced stripping of the ego as your agency is ripped away. Few can understand the psychological trauma that being alone in a dark box plays on the mind. In that reality things that are not real become real. The mind becomes a broken, slave to one primal instinct, to survive.

Michael's horrors in that hell were envisioning the end of the people that the Old Man had told him were sacred. In the moment that directive was compromised there was no reprieve and no salvation. Here he sat, having survived

Earth's invasion, the captivity of mankind, the destruction of

Dyaus and the death of Vorigon. He knew Vorigon hadn't really died and Mastem was most likely alive and still conspiring as well. He honestly felt that when he stepped through that door into the new world it would be a new life, free from the hell he had previously escaped. How wrong his foolish false sense of security had steered him.

Straight into the vipers' pit.

Michael lay staring into nothingness thinking about what lesson he was supposed to learn. It was the knowledge he possessed that hurt him the most. Michael envied the others who died in ignorance to the larger picture. The child who grows up from birth living on cold, unforgiving dirt, eating one meal of sludge for food day and being abused by his family does not know normal, their normal is normal. Without the comparison of a warm soft bed, three meals a day, and the love of those who lift you up how can growth occur? There are those who have always had the warm bed, the meals, and the support and yet they never grow.

Too often it is those who cast the dark shadow of scorn down their noses at the man whose face is mired in the fight, and the good man is labeled the bad man. It is the good men who suffer because they know the meaning of loss, risk, and reward; while the man with everything can never understand anything more than the moments he tries to grow through empathy and rarely action. How can empathy help anyone relate? Can empathy help a person to understand what it's like to be a Buzz Aldrin, Neil Armstrong, or the countless others that have walked on the moon?

How would Colonel Frank Borman, best remembered as the Commander of Apollo 8, the first mission to fly around the Moon, feel if someone used the analogy that they understood perfectly the fear, struggle, and emotion he endured? He envisioned Borman's response, "How, how can you understand?" Empathy says, "Well, I look at the moon every day and night and because I see it and can think about it, I understand your struggle perfectly." With a light inward chuckle, Michael envisioned how hard it was for the survivor to integrate back into society. How many people truly understand what it's like to travel alone in a small box around the moon, knowing that at any moment his life could end?

Who could truly understand? Only those who have endured the same.

Thinking about his own loss and his own life made Michael reminisced about a scripture he had memorized as a boy. He had learned it for personal reasons, not because anyone told him too or that he was prone to the religious experience, rather, because the first time he opened the book it was the first scripture he read. It impacted him, graven on his mind because it applied to his own life. So deeply personal the experience it was in that very moment he knew that there was a higher power speaking to him. Whispering softy to himself he spoke the words, "And I set my mind to know wisdom and to know madness and folly; I realized that this also is striving after wind. Because in much wisdom there is much grief, and increasing knowledge results in increasing pain."

Through every difficult moment he knew that there would be no going back, and if given the opportunity he would change nothing. As hard as that realization was to accept, he would be a vastly different person, and if no one else did or would, he respected himself more for it. He wanted to make a difference; he wanted to be the best, what is the point of being human if he was just like everyone else.

Michael knew his life must matter, how else could he have endured all that had happened? How else could he be enduring this time now trapped in a prison of darkness?

Michael began speaking to himself, as if an imaginary version of himself were sitting in the room, "Don't be afraid to fail, the future is unfolding for you right now, the future is unlimited for you right now, no one knows where you can go, no one knows what you are capable of or what is possible for you, we have the power to change our personal history, changing the direction of our lives, changing our thoughts, expanding our minds. Michael, do not be afraid to fail."

In that moment he became determined to fight to live, he refused to believe this was the end; this was how it would end.

Crawling to the side of the dark space he felt the edges of the corners of the box where the walls met. There had to be a way the box was opened, a weakness. Feeling for where the air was entering he knew this would be the best option for escape.

He hadn't spent time searching for an exit as he spent too much time wallowing in self-pity, the pain that froze him for a time submitting to the moment. He knew the pain was temporary, it may last for a minute, an hour or a year, he knew eventually it would subside. He also knew if he quit it would last forever.

"There it is!" spoke Michael, as he felt a long half inch wide opening at the upper corner of the box. He tried to look through the opening but only darkness, he could not see what was on the other side.

Lying down with his feet pressed against the ceiling, he began kicking over and over. Loud bangs of the pounding echoing. He could feel the surface giving way under the constant pounding of his feet, he was pressing for escape.

Was this really happening, escape possible? The metal bending and cracking under the incessant force, he simply wanted to be free. He knew that with the freedom he would obtain from escape, he could be simply walking into another prison.

With a final kick, a small portion of the corner burst upwards allowing a space large enough to peer through. As Michael pulled himself cautiously through the opening he could see a dimly lit room. The room was beehive shaped, circular with small holes allowing dimly lit light to speckle the floor. Surveying the room, he could see dozens of other box lids still closed circling the perimeter of the room.

Walking slowly, cautiously across the dirt floor he felt the wall covering in holes bringing in the light, it was stone. Peering through one of the holes in the wall he could see a four-foot spiral-like hole that had a bright light on the end. As wind whipped through the hole he knew it was the outside, but where was outside?

In the center of the room was a deep hole roughly 10-feet in diameter that seemed to drop into an empty abyss. That was clearly not a way out. Pacing frantically looking at the other dozen sealed boxes he noticed several had been opened from the outside in a shredded manner. Upon further inspection the metal was torn open in such a way revealing dried blood and the remains of something that had been devoured. Torn from the outside. Turning quickly, he looked around the room, he now knew what this room was, a place of feeding but feeding for what?

Picking up a large piece of metal he went to pry open several of the other still closed boxes. Taking one end he began spearing a corner of the box. Clank, clank, clank the sound echoing through the room.

Michael stopped, the noise was deafening. He tried placing one end of the bar under the edge. Prying with his body as leverage the metal began lifting slowly. Stopping he could hear coming from the hole in the middle of the room, "Da da chuck da da chum". Silently he listened. Again, "Da da chuck da da chum". Moving slowly to the edge of the dark abyss he could hear what sounded like insects moving below. "Da da chuck da da chum" echoing through the room, he now knew it was getting closer.

Looking around the room there was nowhere to hide but the very box he has just escaped. Turning he ran back to the box he was once trapped, grabbing the bent edge of the lid pulling it closed, he held it nearly closed peering out to see what was coming as adrenaline and fear rushed through his body and mind.

"Da da chuck, da da chum, Da da chuck, da da chum"

Closer and closer, "da da chuck, da da chum". Creeping over the edge a massive lobster claw, then another, and another until three large lobster-looking creatures filled the room. The creatures had several large claws on the front with spider legs, a large bulbous head with enormous jaws of seething teeth dripping with saliva. Michael froze in terror; he could not fight these things.

The creatures scurrying to the containers punching the lids rapidly, fangs releasing from the seething jaws. Lids springing into the air, bodies cast to the side of the room. At that moment grabbing one of the bodies, the being was a humanoid lizard. One of the creatures holding the left leg, another the right as a tug of war over began. The third creature with its large lobster claw bursting forward slicing in a downward motion between the legs. The motion repeating, after three strikes the corpse pulled into two pieces, split up the torso. Internal organs spewing onto the floor. Immediately each grabbing a piece of the dismembered body, crawling back into the hole in the center of the room they disappeared into the depths with the sound "da da chuck da da chum" fading into the distance.

Michael dropped low into the container, his hands in his face he needed a moment. The reality of what he had just seen almost too much to bear.

"Are you kidding me?" Michael peered back up into the room before climbing out. Sprinting to the lid he had previously tried opening Michael again began prying as fast as he could, less concerned with the noise he just wanted to open the lid before the creatures returned. With a final heave the lid popped open revealing another lizard type humanoid. Reaching down he grabbed the being by the arms and dragged it onto the floor. Standing silently, he stares at the lizard, watching for any sign of life. The being began to move, it was breathing, its eyes slowly opening. Michael, still holding the metal bar stepped back waiting to see what would happen next. Was this friend or foe?

"Come on, wake up, wake up, wake up" Michael growing impatient, holding the rod like a baseball bat. Michael stood ready for any conflict. The being looked alarmed, glancing to the left, right, up, down, as if in a panic jumping to its feet and rushing to the wall pacing around the circumference of the room. It was looking for something acting as if Michael wasn't even in the room.

Grabbing a piece of metal broken during the extraction by the creatures it began trying to pry open one of the sealed containers. Popping the lid and peering down it moved to the next box, again, opening the lid it crouched down peering into the box. Making a long sigh the being jumped into the container. Slowly an arm, a leg, Michael moved closer. The being was struggling lifting the being in the box out.

As Michael got closer, he was shocked to see a peculiar looking human. Reaching down, grabbing an arm and a leg he helped pull the incredibly large man out of the container. The Lizard being climbing out of the box sat the peculiar man up against the wall before grabbing the piece of metal guarding the being from Michael.

Michael held his bar out, kneeling to the ground he set it on the down. Raising his arms into the air he stood to face the being. The lizard man turned to look at the human before glancing back at Michael. Michael could see the man was what he would consider a Neanderthal. Thick brow, extended forehead, facial features of a human and yet he was not refined in features. He resembled more ape than man. The lizard being then turned and began speaking to the man in an unknown language. The large man quickly rushed to his feet. The two then moving to grab other pieces of metal turned to face Michael.

The large man began speaking to Michael but he could not understand the language. The large man turned to the lizard man and the two began dialoguing. The large man then reached to his left ear digging as if trying to pull something out. Twisting and pulling the man removed a tentacle like insect from his ear. Walking near to Michael he extended his hand out motioning for Michael to take the object. Michael walked to the man and cautiously reached out for the device.

Holding the small device in his hand he could see it was definitely an insect, but not an insect he had ever before seen. A shiny white end, the head, and three long 4-inch tentacles. It resembled a squid, but it was hard like a seashell. The man motioned again, this time for Michael to hold it to his ear.

Michael moved slowly. He was always afraid of things going into his ear. Hesitantly holding the small creature just inches from his ear. Immediately the tentacles diving into his eardrum the device pulled from his hand. It had disappeared within his ear. Immediately Michael was seized upon in immense pain. Hands to his ears, he felt that his head would explode. His nose began dripping blood, the ringing through his head echoing as if it would explode.

Through the pain he thought he could hear speaking. Removing his hands, he listened, "Do you think it will work on him?" "It should work on any being; we need him to help escape from the hive."

Realizing he could hear what the two beings were saying Michael responded, "What did I put in my ear?" The lizard man responding, "It is a listening device. We have used this for centuries to communicate freely among all."

"Where are we?" asked Michael

The massive muscled ape-like man responding, "We in hive." The lizard being responding, "Yes, we need to go!"

"Who are you? Go where? I have looked all around, there are no openings except this black tunnel here that these creatures came out. I am not going down there." Michael was stern with his hands twisting in and out of fists the knuckles crackling and yet his arms straight and rigid. He did not want to go.

"Ares", the ape-man pounding his chest, "This Nergal, my friend. Knows this place, must follow."

"Yes, I know the way. Please follow us, we can help you" responded Nergal.

Turning, without hesitation Nergal jumped into the dark abyss vanishing into the depths below. Michael looking at Ares, still stiff as if molded into the ground, unmovable, "We go down there? But aren't those things down there?"

Ares responding, "Nergal knows this place and how to escape." Immediately, without hesitation,

Ares jumped into the darkness disappearing.

Michael determined to have faith in these two new beings, after all, he had been through worse and what other option did he have? Taking a deep breath, adrenaline coursing through his veins, his heart pounding, he leapt into the darkness.

Free falling Michael could feel cool air below him rushing to meet his skin. With a thunderous splash, he was submerged in water.

Falling into the darkness, not being able to see what was below was unnerving but then hitting black water was terrifying. All he kept thinking, "what's in the water?"

As quickly as he submerged into the water he struggled against the current to reach the surface, he was pulled away.

Michael had been gasping for air, thrusting for survival, fighting just to breathe. Reaching for air. He was being pulled away by the current through an underground river. Just when he thought he had lost the good fight and would drown, he was thrown out of the river into the air.

He was in freefall. In that moment staring at an endless blue sea as he fell thirty feet to the water below. Splashing into the water he surfaced to see Nergal and Ares wading towards the shore. The chalky high cliffs rising above him towered in the air. He could see the opening, the waterfall, the distance near 100 feet. He couldn't believe he had survived.

Wading through the salt water he questioned to himself, "Is this

Tiamat?"

Even though the imagery was so familiar, as if, the cliffs of Dover. Where the line of high kings that ruled Wales for a thousand years had lived, flourished, and faded away. He knew that Earth was lost a long time ago. This must be Tiamat. The hyper crystal blue sky looked like Tiamat's from under the dome and yet… something was different. A hazy pinkish blue covered the horizon. For a moment, the horrors of before were replaced with bliss and beauty.

Michael hastily swam towards shore as it occurred to him there may be many things in the water that would love a free meal. He was terrified of the water.

Walking up the beach towards Nergal and Ares, he could sense that they were panicking, pointing down the beach.

"We must leave here now," spoke Nergal.

Nergal started making way down the long sandy beach that bordered the massive white cliffs. Ares turned and followed unquestioning. Michael began behind them drifting towards the white cliffs. Reaching out with his finger to wipe a smudge of the powder from the stone. Smelling it, tasting it on the tip of his tongue. Salt. The white salt covered cliffs sparkling in the sun, the sand below his feet salt crystals only more refined. The water saltier than any water he had tasted before while swimming he had nearly floated moving at crazy speed. But the breeze whipping off the ocean, across the salt sand touching his face, he could stand in it for an eternity. All Michael could do was close his eyes. For a moment, he was free.

He thought to himself, there must be a purpose. Truly no man has traveled the distances he had covered, and yet as if by the design of Dante's Inferno penning him into a new chapter of horror, he was still here.

Opening his eyes, the weight of reality pressed on his chest. He continued along with Ares and Nergal down the long sandy beach. Nergal wore a leather-like black suit, he was thin with dinosaur-like skin. Facial features in the appearance of a reptile. Eyes, yellow and bulging, opening and closing with two horizontal eyelids. His skin, a brown grey with deep green highlighting the crevasses that separated the scales. Scales that covered his body with a 3-foot tail concealed in the same black leather suit. Nergal had yellow pointy hair that spiked back. If he had not spoken, Michael would have been sure he would be looking at a bi-pedal dinosaur of some velociraptor species.

Ares on the other hand wore animal skins. His hair disheveled with facial hair that was patchy and uneven. His high cheekbones, rough brow ridge, and deeply sunken eyes making him more apelike in appearance than man. The characteristic that stood out the most was the nose and mouth. Protruding like a chimpanzee. With all the apelike features he was still more man than ape but clearly a combination of the two.

Michael addressing Ares, "Where are we going?"

"We must get away from the water before nightfall. That is when the Karkinos come to feed." Ares seemed worried, even at this time spending a great deal of effort constantly watching the shoreline. "Karkinos?" asked Michael. "They rule the sea, and they are the creatures in the hive that feed. Many will come filling the cliffs. If we are here we will die" responded Nergal.

"The lobsters?" Michael questioned as Ares looked perplexed. "Those creatures, the Karkinos, resemble what I know as lobsters. But the lobsters I know are small." Holding his hands up to show the length of two feet.

"That size good eating" spoke Ares. Michael then knew that they were also food here…albeit, very large and intimidating.

"How far do we have to go before we can get off the beach?" questioned Michael

"There is not much daylight left, we have many miles to go." responded Nergal pointing ahead. As he looked to the distance Michael could see the sands gently rising, they would be in fact out very soon.

Nergal then addressed Michael directly, "Where do you come from? I have never seen a being like you."

"It's a long story, another world, another time. Do you know what planet we are on now, is this Tiamat?" Michael spoke with concern in his voice.

"Another world? This is not Tiamat; we are far from Tiamat. This is the Simud" responded Nergal.

"Simud?" questioned Michael sternly, completely surprised. "Where is Simud in relation to Tiamat?" He wanted to gain some insight into where exactly he had been stranded when he was taken captive away from the Chewukon.

Stopping as if puzzled by what Michael was stating, Nergal

walked to Michael. Ares stood to the side looking completely confused by what a Tiamat could be in reference.

"You have been to Tiamat?" questioned Nergal. "Only the High Council of the Seraphim knows of that world, how did you get here? Did the Nephilim bring you? Are you Nephilim?"

"What do you mean when you say Seraphim? Are these your people? Who are the Nephilim?" questioned Michael.

"Those from the outer darkness, the watchers." responded Nergal his hand waving across the sky.

Michael recalled what had happened on Tiamat as the ships arrived. He was momentarily silent.

Approaching a gently sloping hill the escape from the pass along the sea had arrived. What was once a freeing moment turned into being trapped between an unforgiving wall and the dangerous sea filled with flesh eating crustaceans. Here, in the open plains stretching into the distance, he felt optimism rather than pressure.

The three walking to the top of the hill until a large wooded forest could be seen visible in the distance. The men running towards the cover of the trees. As Michael entered the trees he felt a sense of relief sweep over him, he had escaped. But where could he be? These new races of beings, so many questions. Nergal the lizard man and Ares the ape-man. This world that they called Simud, with the large crabs that infested the sea. The forest a deep auburn in color of tall mesquite trees. The air thin but crisp. It was a beautiful place despite the unknowns it could possess.

Turning to face Michael while placing his hand on the shoulder of Ares, Nergal responded. "This is my friend,

Ares. He is a great warrior among my people." We were captured by the Nephilim who tried to kill us for rebelling against their deceptive ways."

Sitting on a fallen tree Michael had now noticed Ares building a fire using a liquid mixed with a power. Seconds later a large fire shot burning embers into the air. The smell of fresh campfire swept through the air. Michael felt relaxed.

"Nergal, tell me more about your people" asked Michael.

"My people are the Seraphim of the Empire of Simud. They reside under the surface because it is too cold on the surface to sustain life. We are the chosen race of Carian, the first world, by the Nephilim. Now we command Simud."

"Nephilim, who are they?" Michael wanting to know more about these mysterious visitors which abducted him after vaporizing an entire civilization at Tiamat. Taking him captive he could now see how he was handed off to the Seraphim to dispose. It was all starting to make sense. He knew this story all too well. Nergal continued speaking to Michael as Ares sat motionless staring into the fire as if lost in a distant memory.

"I am the former High Council Chairman of the Seraphim. Nergal of the House of Aln from Carian. I have tried to change the direction of my people. But they are only interested in one thing, surviving subjugation. We obtain more technology from the Nephilim if we fight back. Come help me. I see within you the desire to have more knowledge."

"My reward was death in a hive of the Karkinos. The High Council is being controlled, and manipulated by the Nephilim. We do not know who the Nephilim are or where they come from. Many of my ancestors ago my people lived on the first world, Carian, the second world from the sun. With our kind we lived for hundreds of millions of years on a lush world of technology. Now we live largely in fear. We live under the surface, once we lived on the surface of our own world." Pausing he looked away, "Carian" softly dropping from his lips. "What type of advantage is it to own a planet if you do own your own skies. The Nephilim own the sky. We created the advanced primate to live on the surface to watch for Nephilim."

"Now, we cower in fear. We spend our lives controlling everything to find sense of self in a crumbling universe where we don't survive. I am not ok with this philosophy. When the Nephilim first appeared, arriving in ships from the sky they began interacting with my ancestors. We were on the brink of destruction."

"They provided my people with a warning that the planet next to our own would be destroyed in a cataclysm. A meteor was heading towards the planet that would eventually wipe out all life, plunging the world into an ice age. They were frantic, and we were desperate. Trapped on our own world, choked by the mistakes of generations since lost to the dust of time."

"An environment impossible for my people to survive, the Nephilim gave my people the technology to escape our own dead world. When the destruction came we came to this world, Simud. The 4th planet from the Sun. The Nephilim have provided us with enough material for space flight and genetic engineering. All of which has occurred in the past 400 years." Michael was stunned silent to what he was hearing. "Now, the Nephilim seem more interested in the ape-man we created than us. We are the remnant of a once mighty nation, a nation that pressed against the boundaries of the stars themselves. The Carian."

"Wait, you mean that 400 years ago the meteor hit Gia killing all life? Was that your original world or another?" asked Michael

"Yes, it was the third world it struck beside our own, we fled here to this world to survive our own world. Moving closer to the Nephilim who really are only interested in the third world we call Gia" responded Nergal.

"I know of this!" Michael exclaiming in exuberance. "It will be hard to explain but I think I know what's going on. I come from another time, another place. Your Gia, I call it Earth. Its where I am from. These Nephilim are beings from other worlds just like this one."

"Have you been back to see Earth, I mean Gia" questioned Michael. He understood, or was beginning to think that he was in the past and not the future, or even another universe. This was Mars, they called Simud. Gia was Earth, but what was Tiamat? The large world positioned between Mars and Jupiter. He recalled how 65-million years into the past a meteor had struck the planet wiping out the dinosaurs and all life. But he also knew many events occurred with many mass extinctions. Where in the timeline he now stood, he had no idea. But this was the right place. Could that be true, or was time twisted and it was only 10's of thousands of years in the past?

Nergal continued, "We started traveling from the planet Simud to see the world thrust into chaos. It is far too volatile for my species to live. We need heat or we die. We have traveled as far as Tiamat, which rests in the gaze of the great red eye. Travel is very slow as it takes one month to travel to Gia and two months to travel to Tiamat where the Nephilim reside doing research. We know they can provide us the technology to travel faster but it is control over our species that then Nephilim truly desire." Pausing to speak with Ares, "Can you find me some grabes?" "Yes, will see" responded Ares before grabbing his metal staff and departing into the darkness. Looking at Michael Nergal continued, "Space travel is not a new understanding for our people. We have once ruled every world in this sea of darkness, it was illuminated with our glow, our greatness." His fist held high clasping as if he knew they were so close and lost it all.

The Nephilim are guiding our race and there is no control to change that, we in return provide them with gold from this planet. We took primates from the planet Tiamat. They have created many different animals and plants on that world from these very beings. We needed workers, not plants."

Pausing, Nergal was speechless. Michael could see that Nergal seemed upset and frustrated. Nergal continued, "I am a bioengineer. We are the greatest engineers that have existed. We have so many that are created for this purpose. They genetically engineered Seraphim-Primate hybrids, like Ares."

Michael immediately cut him off, "Primate? Why would you call him a Primate? Have you seen any other men like me?"

"He is a primate because that is what was used to create his species. You forget, the hearing device in your mind changes and interprets even my language into one that you understand and yet I may not have recollection of the words you hear. It is the same for me. As for other men, yes, they live on Tiamat with the Nephilim but they are not like you." Pointing to Ares he continued, "But neither is he. We use these primates to mine for gold and be our workers on the surface since escaping from the home world in the past. They are our eyes on the sky. These workers live on the surface of Simud while we reside within the planet."

"Why do you live inside of the planet?" asked Michael inquisitively. "It's not by choice, trust me, if we could advance beyond the restrictions that bind us to the planet. If we simply had 100 monkey's from Tiamat we could just leave ourselves. Enough genetic material to do whatever we desired. It's the atmospheric pressure. Our home world, Carian's atmosphere, was once much denser and thicker than this planet. We can only survive for short periods of time on the surface. Which is why we must get into the interior first thing tomorrow morning. The structure of the planet Simud."

Interrupting Nergal, Michael questioned, "You mean Mars?" Nergal continued, "This world, Simud, yes as you say Mars, the fourth world from the Sun. The interior offers pressure that helps us to maintain our internal biorhythm."

"These primate men once worshipped us as Gods, we having

been their creators. They ruled the surface with the technology we provided. But then the Nephilim started appearing to them."

"The Nephilim ships released a growth agent into the atmosphere. It misted through the air like a virus infecting all the hominid workers. Their genetic evolution-becoming advance with every breath. As time went on the hominids began thinking for themselves and some turned on us. These were the Wars of Simud."

They no longer believe we were Gods. They saw us as enemies and sought to destroy us. There has been a war on this planet ever since and we have been trapped here by the Nephilim. Stripped of our ability to utilize their technology, too free ourselves."

"Many of my kind thought to destroy them." Pointing to Ares. "But others, like myself, wondered about the ethical implications of engineering an autonomous species for control. They had become aware. In this awareness, we became aware. Had we not faced our own plight against the Nephilim it may have never matter and yet we want freedom from the Nephilim. We sought the freedom of Ares kind from the Nephilim before it was too late for us both."

"Nergal, I know this will be hard to believe, but I believe that I come from the future where my race of humans is being controlled by advanced races of beings from distance galaxies and parallel universes. Some of which might be these Nephilim."

"Where I am from, this planet Simud is uninhabited and Tiamat doesn't even exist. An advanced being sent me here, I just can't figure out why yet."

"This is the same thing we experienced there, one race rising to escape into space only to meet its masters waiting in the darkness to enslave and seek dominion over them. The bane of less advanced species."

Michael continued, "But there are others who protect life, who seek to preserve all life. I have seen them, and it is them who have sent me here. Let me ask you a few questions about these Nephilim."

"Are they gray in appearance? Large black eyes? Do they travel in saucers?"

"Yes, they are tall thin grey praying mantis. The ancients they say." Nergal responded hesitantly.

"I know who these Nephilim are, they are called The Celestials. I believe that I have dealt with them in my timeline" responded Michael.

Nergal responded, "The enemy of my enemy is my friend."

Michael seemed perplexed, how he had been sent backwards, the final words from the Old Man that one chapter had ended and another would begin. It weighed heavily upon his mind. He had said Michael would protect them. Was that why he was here, to find a way to overcome and preserve the human species in this timeline. The unknown roll of the dice so that the future would be, as it should? It was perplexing to think about but he knew the first thing he needed to do was get inside Simud.

In the darkness that surrounded them he could here movement coming in the distance. Voices. Glowing green orbs appeared through the small sagebrush like trees.

Appearing out of the darkness was a contingency of eight lizard men holding staffs with glowing green larva attached to their ends. The glowing larva caught Michael's attention immediately because they looked like giant glowworms. The toys he had seen as a child. Every so often they would pulsate emitting light that would become very bright and then slowly diminish before repeating. Michael counted 10 seconds between pulsations.

One of the Lizards came forward as a representative of the group. Nergal approached him with a strange greeting. Spikes springing forward, tails rising high, they nodded in a circular pattern. They began walking in a circle with their tales embracing and their hands straight out touching at the palm. The hands were only three large fingers like Nergal. Nergal turning to Michael and Ares, "Hurry we must leave now, before the Nephilim arrives. These are my friends and they will take us to a safe place below." Turning they moved into the darkness. In time Michael could see the adjacent mountain range.

2

KULKUKAN

It had been thirty days since Michael left the "Old Man" to live among the Chewukon. The Chewukon were as close to Native American's Michael could imagine and most resembled the Hopi from the southwest. At least in the images with his mind.

The Chewukon were peaceful in every way, no concept for conflict, always soft spoken and lived in an almost graceful humanity. With the exception of a few items that helped process raw meat and their peculiar instruments for hunting, they had no technology.

Michael had stumbled into the camp after walking through the door hesitant about his safety. The first thing that happened when the people had become aware of him was a group of older native women. They approached him placing an immaculately woven blanket around his shoulders. He was welcomed to sit at their fire.

The Chewukon treated him with no disregard, as if he were one of their own. When he met their leader, a bearded old native it struck him as odd because he had never seen a bearded native. He called himself Ququmatz and he referred to his people as the Chewukon.

Ququmatz spoke of star people who had brought them to this place to protect them until the time came that they would go to a new world. To Michael, he was not sure if he understood correctly, but based upon his dealings with the many alien beings he knew more than likely even here there were accounts of interactions with beings from the sky. After all they were here and the sky was there.

Michael had drifted easily into the routine of life as a helper to the natives of this strange new world. He relished the calmness and the peace. The rumblings were still present to look outwards, he would in time, but now the stability mattered most. The journey ahead, not so much. The staple diet of the Chewukon was fish. Though they hunted, it was rare; most all food was either fish, plants, or a form of wheat.

The wheat surprised Michael because it was something that was unique to Earth. The fish were different than anything he had seen, they resembled a cross between a carp and salmon.

Michael's days were spent learning the language and helping build new homes in the cliffs. In his free time, he focused on mapping the land and trying to determine where he had been placed, he had no idea.

Michael knew he was not on Earth for a few reasons. The main difference, smoking gun, was the lack of a moon in the sky; in fact, there were no moons or objects in the sky. Just a deep blue that sparkled at times like refractions off crystal.

The other thing that he noticed. The sun in the sky was smaller almost dimmed out by the crystal refraction of the blue sky. Nothing like the clear sky he had remembered on Earth. The temperatures were cooler hovering in what he suspected 60-70 degrees. For all intents and purposes Michael was in a paradise.

Ququmatz was what they called a great fisherman. Ququmatz carried a spear with him at all times. The spear was unlike any the other Chewukon carried; it released a vibration when placed in the water. Immediately all fish rose to the surface.

He would use the same manner with food. When placed in the ground large wooly mammoths within 100 yards would fall to the ground dead. Michael marveled at the technology.

Looking at Ququmatz, Michael touched the spear then held his arms out questioning where he had obtained this staff. The old bearded native simply pointed to the sky. This made Michael very nervous, as his only experience with beings from the sky was life altering and dangerous. The people considered it a sacred artifact from their ancestors. Michael was intrigued at the technology and marveled at how they only took what they needed.

With the advanced technology they could operate without limits killing everything. Something he had seen so many humans do on the Earth. He remembered how technology had only served to divide mankind, to distract them. Those who had withholding and leveraging from those who had not.

He remembered all the advances back on Earth and questioned within his heart why mankind would not seek to eliminate poverty, starvation, and homelessness. He often questioned why mankind hadn't made food and shelter an entitlement, had they, the possibility existed of a united front against the invaders rather than a divisive bickering peoples that met their doom.

When Michael had approached Ququmatz further about where the device had come he mentioned again that there was a great taking and the staff was given by the sky.

Michael wondered what the great taking could be. He wondered what that meant. Again, fear began to rise within him as he knew all too well how sentient beings had enslaved and destroyed humanity. Was this part two?

Ququmatz and Michael spent nearly every day together. Ququmatz considered Michael one of the great mountains sent from the Great Spirit. Michael could not figure out why he was referred to as a mountain by the old leader. Since Michael had come to these people the powers he had before were gone. He was just a regular man. As if by design he understood their language, in a way it was broken English. By the powers of the Old Man that sent him hear or simply luck, he understood the language. These were questions he most likely would never know.

The Chewukon had spread across the land in dwellings carved into the mountain cliffs. The Mountain cliff homes were carved using what looked like a pen. By all intents and purposes that was what it was, a pen. It was a sacred object to the Chewukon that was kept in a chamber. It was not worshipped or treated as a deity, but they would have a ceremony each time it was removed from its place of keeping and when they returned it.

One morning Michael was determined to walk as far in one

direction as he could. He had hoped to gain a better understanding of the land and see if he would meet other tribes. He had let the old chief know what direction he would be going, the forbidden forest.

The old chief seemed troubled and didn't want him to go. Michael insisted. Finally relenting, the chief gave him a staff with a shard of purple crystalline strapped to the end. It was a staff he had not seen before. He touched a rock with the tip and the rock fractured in two. It was a weapon. Why would he need a weapon when everything he had known among these people was extreme peace and non-hostility? The forbidden forest, how had it escaped him? Obviously called forbidden for a reason.

Leaving the mountain dwellings, he began heading towards where the sun would be setting. He had wanted to explore this part of the land anyways because across the wheat fields was this forest the people never entered and seemed to avoid. The forest was gigantic, stretching into the distance as far as his eye could see as viewed from the high cliff side homes.

As Michael neared the tree line cutting sharply adjacent to the fields of wheat. He saw the true size of the trees. Not unlike the redwoods of northern California, every tree was over 400 foot tall. Moving through the forest the sound became silent. Deathly silent. The canopy dimming, the light to near dusk.

As Michael moved through the forest he could sense the once peaceful calm of the Chewukon was replaced with an earie silence. It was simply too quiet. It was so silent that it did not seem real. No wind rustling the leaves. No branches breaking or swaying in the air. No birds. No insects. Could this really be a sterile environment? If so, it was by design. This worried Michael deeply.

This was the forbidden forest, and he was determined to see it to the other side. What was the other side? What horrors could possibly be awaiting him?

He could have stayed with the Chewukon in a peaceful society perhaps for the remainder of his days. Yet, the explorer in him, the seeker in him, pressed forward. Seeking answers that he did not have to questions he did not know.

After walking for the entire day, he could only speculate the distance. If he had walked 15-minutes per mile for the duration of 10 hours he could have traveled a distance of 30-40 miles and yet the forest had no end in sight and he needed to find shelter as the sun was setting.

In the entire distance not a bug, not a bird, not a sound. Just the perfectly pristine forest. As if swept clean. The forest floor stretching endlessly into the distance. No needles from the trees, no bark shavings. The ground frozen in time. Perfect cleanliness overshadowed by the massive trees. How could that be unless it all fabricated, on a scope he could actually imagine. Anything was possible after the things he had seen.

Surveying the area Michael contemplated the best place to set up camp. Moving towards one of the large trees he could see part of the massive roots protruding from the ground revealing a hollowed cavity within the tree.

The inside of the tree was massive. The large trees were in fact redwoods, at least he believed or some distant relative. How can redwoods be here? Having the opportunity to review the bark, which he shaved off to use to help make a fire it resembled in absolute perfect shape and form the red fibrous cedar-like material of a sequoia. The inside of the tree measured at 15 paces across.

Digging a hole in the center of the hollowed out room he stripped tinder from the tree to make a fire. He knew this would be the material used to let larger wood ignite. Using the staff that Ququmatz gave him he split tree limbs to use as kindling. Striking the tip of the spear against a rock sparks ignited the tinder and Michael slowly added the kindling. Keeping the fire small he could feel the tree cave heating up as the temperatures outside began to fall.

Darkness was upon him.

Sitting by the fire Michael began processing the previous experience on Dyaus. What had become of the man in black? Something about that moment, it seemed too easy. Vorigon had been defeated without any effort and a part of him knew that Vorigon had not been destroyed. He might never know.

Pulling out some of the fish he had brought with him he tore strips and began eating while surrounded in the silence of the massive forest. Flashbacks began ringing through his mind. The zombies of Earths invasion. The infected who were scratched by the zombies. The weapon that encapsulated the infected crushing them into marble sized containers for disposal. It flashed across his mind over and over. The travels, the journeys, the fear, the invigoration, being free. It had been a long road to this point of seemingly insecure security and solidarity in the journey that led to the forests of the Chewukon. Rolling out the blanket provided by the people Michael drifted off to sleep.

Awaking to screams that echoed through the forest Michael sprung to his feet. What the hell could that be? Grabbing the staff he quickly bound tinder to the tip lighting it on fire. He slowly emerged from the hollow of the tree. The next minute he could see large beasts advancing upon some unknown machines with purple glowing lights. The machines were tearing into some large creature less than 100 feet from his position as others were battling the machines.

As Michael moved closer he could see the huge beings. Sasquatch, only bigger. In that moment he put the fire out. Michael was an observer. The fight, however, did not end there. The injured sasquatch lying on the ground helpless as a half dozen giants began attacking the machines.

Twisting and pulling the legs of the machines, the lights being torn out, they fought. The machines sought to bind them or tear them to pieces. Michael could not believe what he was seeing. A massive ship then arrived dropping more machines with glowing lights which slammed to the ground opening an offensive against the large sasquatch beings.

One of the sasquatch had stumbled towards Michael's location. A machine following had clamped onto the back of the massive beast with a whirling sound tearing into its flesh. The large sasquatch let out a blood curdling scream of agony. He had waited long enough, Michael running at full speed began stabbing the machine with the spear. The large robot blew up blasting Michael backwards slamming into a tree.

He lay half unconscious staring at the fight, as a louder yell came from the distance. A massive 20-foot-tall sasquatch running full speed towards the large collection of machines colliding with such force they exploded to the ground lifeless.

The smaller machines surviving the collision scurried off into the distance as if in fear. Writhing and exhausted this large hairy bipedal sasquatch fell to its knees. The others surrounding it to help it and the injured away.

As the original creature lay on the ground, writhing and

sometimes roaring, the others who survived the attack gathered around and picked it up. The largest sasquatch turning towards Michael until eye contact was made. It moved instantly towards him. He stood still unmoving. It kneeled down peering into his eyes less than 6 inches from his face.

Michael was exhausted and he could tell so were the Sasquatch. The large sasquatch lifting Michael to his feet. With a few grunts turning and moving back towards the group of sasquatch. Michael moved quickly back to the hollowed tree hiding against the inner bark. He slowly sank to the ground. Another conflict, another survival.

They were the largest sasquatch of any kind he had ever seen or imagined. The machines, what were they doing here?

How could machines be here? Why were they trying to destroy the sasquatch and who was this large sasquatch that towered above the rest who had lifted him up from the ground when he could have stomped him from existence. Why had they spared him?

Was it because he saved one? Speaking in whoops and wales the creatures picked of the fallen comrade before disappearing into the ground. How could they just vanish beneath the surface where the ground seemed rock hard?

He could see the large being reaching down to the ground before exposing an entrance. Others seemed to sink into the soil until they were unseen. As quickly as the ordeal had begun it was over but Michael's faith in the peace he had once know, it had vanished.

Michael sat the rest of the night in silence unable to sleep. Trying to figure out what he had just witnessed and why it had happened. It was all in the blink of an eye. Drifting off to sleep Michael was again woken to the sound of sweeping.

Peering outside of the tree Michael could see the purple lights reemerging from the darkness. How long had he been asleep?

His head ringing from the slam against the tree, he most likely had a concussion. He felt sick, uneasy his head pounding in pain.

As the machines neared him he could see they were cleaning the dirt in a sweeping motion with the sound of a street sweeper. This was why the forest floor was so immaculately kept but what could they be?

Watching them move by in the hundreds he sat silent. Across the forest floor and into the darkness, as quickly as they appeared, they were gone.

In the morning, Michael moved cautiously towards the spot where the attack had occurred. On the ground was nothing. It was as if nothing had occurred.

The very place he was sure the massive sasquatch had descended into the ground was as hard as rock. It defied logic. Had it even happened?

Packing his things Michael continued his journey towards the other side of the forest. On Earth he remembered the stories of Sasquatch. Michael thought he once saw a sasquatch on a hillside at Waha Lake, Idaho. The big foot would simply vanish without a trace. Undetectable and yet from every corner of the globe they were seen. Known as Yeti, Timber Giants, and the Hairy Man.

These were many times larger than any of the sasquatch he had ever heard about on Earth. The giant sasquatch had just stared into his eyes and then left him in peace. Obviously these were benevolent creatures or at least it seemed they respected his help. They did not engage him in conflict. They engaged the machines that were attacking. Here we go again, he thought, always drawn towards conflict. After several hours Michael could hear for the first time the sound of rushing water in the distance.

This invigorated him and his pace increased until almost frantically he was in full sprint towards what appeared to be an end to the forest. As Michael neared the edge he stopped more cautiously moving, staying in the thick foliage of the forest. Moving slowly towards the tree line what he saw next shocked him to the core. For a moment brought hopelessness back into his heart.

"Why would you do this to me?" He screamed into the air.

Stepping slowly out into a flat dirt opening the reality of the situation became clear. Lifting his hand to press against the barrier he was face to face with a clear glass wall. Rising into the air he could see that a glass-like barrier trapped him and seemed to extend in all directions. Looking through the glass the ground was sheet metal grey. With Machines moving back and forth like a highway. In the distance he could see glass domes in all directions with other green habitations enclosed within them.

Turning to put his back against the glass he slid to the ground. "Bio-dome." Where the hell had he gone?

Machines rising into the air moving back and forth in all

directions. He was again a prisoner, trapped in a cage. A zoo on a strange world. What else could it be? Before he had time to mourn his captivity, to think about his next move, red-beaming lights pierced down upon him. The machines had spotted him.

Hovering in the air, the giant sentinel tentacles waiving in the air. They were scanning him top to bottom. Loud sirens emanating everywhere screaming alarm through the air. Michael rose and began running at full speed back into the cover of the forest. Looking back, he could see the machines move through the glass capable of escaping the force field that held him hostage at will.

Seeking knowledge had led to answers he was not prepared to accept. Why hadn't he just stayed in the village? Why hadn't he fought against his compulsions to "know" all things? Why did he have to explore everything?

Here he was running from machines that obviously knew he was not meant to be in this place. Heart pounding. Mind racing. Sweat protruding. He was in a race for his life. The machines on his tracks with red beams scanning the area would surely kill him.

As Michael moved at all out speed he immediately fell through the soil into the under earth below. Slamming onto the ground of a tunnel he could see he hadn't fallen. He had been pulled down by a sasquatch. Escaping the clutches of the machines, did his plight just get worse? He was again face to face with the sasquatch.

The sasquatch offering its hand clasping Michaels own. Raising to his feet the being urged him to follow. Moving through the dark corridors dimly lit by glowing stones pressed into the walls. Michael could tell they were descending deeper and deeper into the ground through the corridor.

After a 400 foot of descent into the tunnel an opening into a large corridor with a lift. "A lift?" Michael stated openly. How could an elevator like structure be here? The tall fifteen foot being never spoke, simply operating controls on the lift.

Walking onto the lift Michael watched as the sasquatch removed a chip and placed it into an opening. The caged structure began its descent below as electricity began wrapping around the structure. Looking down it seemed an endless pit into darkness.

After dropping at an incredible speed Michael noticed the electricity beaming around the lift increasing. A portal opened beneath the lift. They were descending through a wormhole-like opening until it emerged revealing light below and solid stone above.

When the lift descended into the light he could see a new world filled with trees and mountains. The sky was made of glowing rock arching to reveal another subterranean dome. Were they inside the planet or did they teleport to another planet or dimension?

He was beyond confused but looking around he could see this was a massive cavern. The sasquatch walked to a plate on the wall next to the lift pulling out what looked like a flash drive that was inserted into a control module connected to the lift. This must be the device to operate the lift. The tall hairy being motioning him to follow. They moved towards a massive tree city that encompassed the center of the cavern.

"Where are we" asked Michael. The tall hairy being not saying a word, just gliding through large ferns that lined the pathway. They were heading to the village in the center of the cavern.

In the center of the cavern was a city unlike any of the numerous places he had seen. It was filled with trees, but not trees like the redwoods. Trees that grew into structures as if programmed. The city lit by the rock above which glowed brilliant fire yellow and yet it was not blinding like the sun nor hot like fire. He could see what looked like movement above the ceiling. It appeared like clear glass or crystalline of some form revealing magma burning and twisting above it.

His hand brushing against the ferns he followed the giant until he could see many giants. As he passed by they stopped staring at him.

The city resembling three large circles. The outer circle separated from the inner circle by a lake. The inner circle a large tree dome.

Michael noticed the other beings. He could hear whispering. He was able take out a few distinct sounds. What he thought he heard was, Plaedian. He heard this word at least six times.

Looking back the large cliffs revealed containing the elevator lifts numbered in the dozens. Sasquatch entering and exiting. The elevators shooting up and appearing down to the surface continuously.

Michael had been so focused looking at the hundreds of big foot, the ceiling and the surrounding lifts he failed to realize he had reached a large gate. Woven with roots into decorative designs it had been grown from the ground beneath him. It was marvelous to behold such craftsmanship. Pink flowers sprouting from the twisting roots. The arching gate revealing the first large circular city. Within the walls the city was filled with simple tree houses.

No canopy on the trees. The ground paved with perfectly circular quarter-sized pieces of wood. Stopping to kneel down he could feel these too were roots that had grown to form the most amazing roadway he had seen. This was a wooded city by design engineered.

The first circular ring of dwellings was only one hundred meters long. At the water barrier there were many of the sasquatch pulling out oval blobs that resembled loaves of bread but moving like maggots. This was their food source as he saw many bite into them. Green slime dripping and falling to the ground.

Michael tried to avoid eye contact as he felt like a bug that they could squash at any time. The village of giant sasquatch seemed serene and in harmony. It was simple with ornate wood dwellings.

Michael had again been consumed with the moment. He had arrived at the second circle of buildings across the second bridge leading to the center of the city. He stood at the door of the large dome. The dome rose high above as tree trunks served as pillars twenty feet apart. Separated by massive leaves that grew perfectly to show a glowing green roof. It was a living building. The sasquatch removed its chip inserting it into another key slot. The leaves immediately dissolved revealing an opening.

The large space within the dome was empty. A swirling ball of solid grey material floated in the middle of the room. The sasquatch then stepping to the side revealed something so startling that Michael took several steps backwards. It was the old man.

"How can you be here?" Michael questioned stunned to see this being here. The old man moved slowly towards Michael before reaching out to ask for his spear. "I am not giving this to you!"

"Oh young man, I am not going to take it from you. I need to review the chard." Again motioning for the staff.

Michael refused, "I will not give you the staff until you tell me why I am here, why you are here!" Immediately two large sasquatch moved towards Michael to take the spear from him by force. The old man motioned them off. "That will be unnecessary, let him hold the staff. I guess I do have some explaining."

The old man spoke again, "What is your name? Have we met before?"

"Of course we have met, it was you who sent me here. Don't play games with me." The frustration felt in the emotion of his words. The old man simply turned towards the spinning sphere in the center of the room responding, "The Great Spirit."

Turning back to Michael, "Your name son?"

"So you never sent me here? My name is Michael Bethios."

"No, we have not met but I have a feeling you have met the Great Spirit. It is he who has sent you here and now it would seem our paths have crossed."

"Follow me." Turning the man motioned Michael to the spinning orb in the center of the room. The orb spinning at a rapid rate counter clockwise. The old man spoke, "This world is dying, and once the heart of the world stops all will be lost."

Michael wanted answers. "So, where are we?"

"We are in the center of the great mother of the Chiye Tanka. My name is Kulkukan. I am the guardian of the Chiye Tanka, our Elder Brothers."

Michael was confused. "We are in the center of the planet? I saw what happened outside, what was the glass barrier? Who were those machines?"

The old man answering, "Those are the Nephilim from the Nibiru."

"The Nibiru?" Questioned Michael, he had heard that name before many times. The old man called in an unknown language to one of the large Chiye Tanka to bring him a long beaded neckless that was coiled onto the ground beneath the spinning orb.

Michael noticed around the old man's waste was a satchel filled with the grey chips that were used to power the lifts. As Kulkukan ran his fingers across the many different colored beads, it was as if he were reading some form of brail or historical recording system. Covered in a feather cloak of many colors he continued, "Awe, here it is, many seasons ago this was the new world of the Chiye Tanka when the Sky Father brought my people here to live. The Nephilim came from the darkness and brought their technology to our world. At first we cohabited in peace. But as their appetite for research expanded they sought dominion over us. Isolated and trapped my people were forced into large domes on the surface. Forcing myself and the Chiye Tanka to retreat into the heart of our great mother. Then they started creating unknown creatures and the experiments expanded. So many of my people have perished. Those left are isolated and imprisoned in one of the many structures on the surface."

Placing his arm on one of the Chiye Tanka he continued, "These are not creatures, or beasts, they are our elder brothers. They trace their origins to the sky father who brought us here on the wave of sound. They are a tribe of ancients who have served as guardians. The trees, all life on this world emanates from their presence. We have retreated here to this place to avoid conquest by the dark ones from the empty sky."

Kulkukan placed the beads back into a coil on the ground.

"Michael, you cannot leave this place. It is not safe on the surface."

Stunned at such a unilateral decision. "So you will just hold up helpless here trapped in your own self-made prison? You do not control me, I have to figure out where I am and why I was sent here. I was not sent here to hide, to give up in willing submission. You do realize that there are world destroyers out there in space that will find you. You are only delaying the inevitable. You do realize that?"

The old man seemed incapable of grasping the true magnitude of the situation. Michael continued, "You seem like a man refusing to accept the present. Living in the past thinking that life will improve. It can't improve, it never does."

Michael remembered when the Europeans first discovered America. They approached the natives with the mentality of divine providence. While the native sought peace they were quickly slaughtered in their inability to adapt and accept the judgment that befell them. Here he was with another group of people who thought they could simply wait out the storm. Oblivious to the fact the it would eventual erase them from the timeline. Michael knew that story all too well. He was a descendant of natives. The most persecuted and discriminated group to ever walk the face of the modern world. The forgotten people who never received their reparations. There were no reparations left to give. Michael pondered, when cultures clash it is the infantile that crush the wise. This was the case with the history of the natives of North America. A land of the free, offering hope, a new beginning for everyone except the native man. Why was this so? He often wondered if the fundamental foundation ingrained into each native was not conducive to progress. The concept of leverage foreign. Where is leverage over another if a blanket is free, if food is free, if shelter were given freely. Who would rape and pillage his or her own mother or withhold from a brother or a sister? It was a holy mindset that threatened the very existence of those who have and those who have not. He felt it was a sad tale of the destruction of the only people who deserved to have dominion over the Earth, because they never saw it as dominion.

He then addressed the old man directly. "Kulkukan, we have to leave this place, we have to find a way to stop this madness. You may choose to stay here in your coffin until the end comes but I am leaving."

"That is impossible son. The only time we can go to the surface is at night. We cannot penetrate the barriers that they have covered over the domes on the surface. Either we are trapped here or we are trapped there, it makes no difference." Kulkukan was indifferent.

Michael recalled a quote by Anna Freud and recited it to the old man, "We live trapped, between the churned-up and examined past and a future that waits for our work."

"Kulkukan, I was told when I came to this place by the Great Spirit to help you. He said I would protect you. I need you to trust me. What happens to these people and the Chiye Tanka when you die? They are then doomed. Let's use this time to find a way to escape. From what I know they have ships, if we can obtain a ship we can try to find another world and escape."

Kulkukan was unmoved. "This is our world. For now, you will reside here. We can't let you leave this place, there is too much at risk, too much to lose. My job is to protect these people for one more day, not make risks for personal desires. Does the tree question its place in the forest even when the tree faces being hewn down or plucked from the soil? Does it move or does it fear? It stands silent to its last final moment. Grateful for its mission to shelter the bird, protect the beetle, and when the time comes it willing provides the resources to sustain others. This is the way of the Chiye Tanka, the way of the Great Spirit. I am the tree of this forest and my job is to stand my place until the time comes when I will leave. It's the way things have always been. One day they will leave and we will reclaim this world."

Michael understood what he was saying, what a noble way to live. He respected the Old Man for staying true to his principles in face of annihilation.

"That is naive, to say the least, they will take everything there is on this planet. Those impenetrable barriers are called metal. Add in the glass domes and this planet is being choked to death. What will you do when this entire world dies? Well, that is not good enough for me! My life is my own. There's no fate but what we make for ourselves." Michael stated sternly squaring up with one of the sasquatch.

Kulkukan continued, "The heart of the Mother here" pointing to the spinning ball, "will stop if that is true and then neither us nor them can live here and perhaps that is the way of the Great Spirit. From death comes life. Let me not impede your decision." Reaching into his satchel he removed a chip before handing it to Michael. "You are free to go. Who am I to bind you and hold you captive from your destiny?"

Michael took the chip, before turning towards the door. "I will be back to help you escape this madness. This is madness Kulkukan. There is no happiness in submission, no freedom in prison." The old man crossing his arms with a slight grin of approval, as if he knew something that Michael was unaware. Something about the old man seemed so pure, loving, and genuine. What it would be like to live life unconcerned with life, death, or the barriers that bind and cast a man into captivity. It was a commendable way to live.

Motioning to one of the Chiye Tanka the Kulkukan spoke, "Ste ya ma, escort this man to the lift but do not go onto the surface."

Michael and the sasquatch turned and returned towards the lift. As Michael stood at the entrance to the lift, he thought to himself again, this was the second time he has had the opportunity to live the remainder of his life in peace. Why did he care so much? What drove him into conflict? He wished he knew why he thrived on the unknown. Stepping into the lift the tall being looked down at him. For the first time Michael could see clearly, this was not a big foot. The sasquatch was a native with facial hair and body hair. It was a tribe of native-type people but huge. The lift raised into the light of electricity revealing a conduit that led to the surface.

Emerging from within one of the large trees that had been hollowed out Michael exited the lift stepping out into the wilderness. Not two steps out and everything went black. A large canvas was netted around him. The sounds of machines hovering in the air. Waiting for his arrival. In an instant he was trapped. He was taken.

3

SIMUD

Nergal had led Michael with the group of his kind into a cave system that winded through the depths below the mountains. A long narrow tunnel carved into the red rock of the planet Mars.

The journey was difficult. They pressed through narrow corridors cut with precision deep into the planet. It was much more difficult than it had been while on Tiamat when he was taken to Kulkukan. The lizard men weren't as large as the sasquatch native men.

The group reached a dead end where the rock was smooth with hieroglyphics surrounding the perimeter.

Michael too unnerved to speak watched as Nergal moving to the characters began pressing them. With each touch they glowed a brilliant fluorescent green. In a jerking motion the stone slab slowly turning revealing a corridor on the other side. Standing in that corridor were beings like Ares among seraphim reptilians. Running forward one of the women embraced Ares.

Ares separated from the group as Nergal asked Michael to join him down the corridor. Ares spoke very little following all commands of Nergal. When he did respond it was in broken sentences that were incomplete and forced.

"Where are they going Nergal?" Asked Michael in reference to Ares, the women and the many primate looking men with him. "They are going to the place where their group is encamped."

Nergal began speaking again, "Too long I've lived, too much I've seen. This planet, our host, once so wild and unknown." As if reaching for the next words to say. "We've mapped it, conquered it, arranged it on a grid, risen to almighty rulers of the cosmos, only to have it snatched away as if we were only feeble infants. Michael, there is a war, a war between the Seraphim and the Nephilim."

Nergal was a leader. His demeanor changed upon entry home. Would he expect anything different for himself if he could go home? The pride of family to the heart of any conscious being. Nergal continued as many more stood closely to listen to his words. "We were once so much more than we are now. Scouring and hiding in the shadows. Worms under the feet of giants of time. What little knowledge we possess, having obtained from seeds of information from the enemy. I want to show you something."

Motioning Michael towards an opening that revealed a cavity in the planet many times larger than the one he had seen on Tiamat where Kulkukan and the Elder Brothers resided. Filled within the catacomb, honeycombed dwellings that covered the entire surface. Lizard-beings were moving effortlessly across the ceiling, the walls and the deep valley below.

A metallic looking platform rose before Michael and Nergal. Stepping onto it, the platform moved without sound towards a smoke stack pumping clouds of vapor into the air. Below it a large building.

"We are preparing for war. We will retake our world and our kind will rise again with the help of Ares. But you, you are different and we need you to help us. "

"Do I have a choice?" responded Michael

"No. You do not. But out of respect for assisting in my escape from the hive I am requesting you choose to assist us in our rebirth."

What other option did he have? Michael responded as only he knew how. "What do you need me to do?"

Nergal looked pleased at that response. "I would like to have you examined. To review what you are made of, to see if you contain within you the ingredients that we need." He paused before continuing. "To create what must be created to gain our freedom."

"What type of examination are we talking about?"

"In this room is a chamber, it analyzes the building blocks of all elements. Allows us to extract the code we need to synthesize life. We have run out of this material, what you see, these primate men you see, they will never amount to produce what we need. We need building blocks. Their predecessors are flawed and lacking in free genetic material that can be manipulated. Therefore, their intelligence is limited, their ability to react, adapt, to become anything more than a servant is hindered. Unfortunately, without us, without leadership they would only find extinction had the Nephilim not advanced them. We must fight back, we need new building blocks that the Nephilim have never seen. I think they have never seen anything like you."

In the center of the room was a large black egg. Opening steam emanated from the edges revealing pink flowing worms covering the entire surface of its interior.

"You will enter here, it will close, and we will analyze the fabric of your creation. Any luck reproducing the building blocks that are contained within you. It is the material we lack, that we desire. If we are successful, and I think we will, imagine armies of intelligent beings such as yourself. Even more powerful intelligences that could wage war on our behalf. Imagine the ability of my kind to walk freely outside the confines of these caves?"

"You are looking for my DNA, aren't you? Responded Michael.

"DNA?" Questioned Nergal.

Michael responding as quickly as the previous remark. "The genetic make-up that is contained in every cell that organizes matter that programs matter for me. I will do this but only because I want to find the bastards who captured me. To see them fall. Before I met you I was on the Tiamat, it was covered in domes that contained people like me, well, not like me but not like Ares either. In the center of that planet is a man named Kulkukan, and an army of giants. They are travelers from another universe who used to rule that planet before it was overtaken by these Nephilim."

Michael pushed for more answers. "So you said, they are rebuilding the planet Earth or Gia, why?"

"Why do you think? So they can have the planet for themselves.

That is why. We lack genetic material, the material we have is not viable for this task. When you use material to create a being of life, then use that being's genetic material to create another, it becomes unstable. Diluted even on the macro scale the micro imperfections are visible. The Nephilim will not provide us with any more material." Smarted Nergal inquisitively before continuing. "You have been inside that world? So it is true, this is where they are obtaining the material needed to build life. We must obtain access."

Michael could see between the lines, "Ok, I will do this, and you are confident I won't be harmed?"

"You will not be harmed, but you will need to remove all of your clothes, and the sechuim communication organism".

Pulling out a smooth black stone he held it to Michael's ear. Instantly the entity released from his ear wrapping around the stone like the shell of an egg wrapping the yoke.

Stepping into the pink structure the tentacles began latching onto his legs and his arms. As the capsule closed the tentacles attached to every part of his body. Sharp stings of needles were felt across his entire body.

From the outside Nergal moving quickly. A large collection of reptilians operating the mass of electrical equipment that surrounded the room began pressing the instruments.

The instruments resembling plants were not like the electrical equipment used on Earth in Michael's past.

This truly was an alien technology.

Inside the machine Michael was screaming in agony but could not make a noise. He was paralyzed, but felt every bit of the pain. Tentacles pressing down his throat, fluid filling his extremities, he felt as though he was being torn into pieces.

As quickly as it had begun, it was over. The tentacles releasing Michael collapsed within the machine resting upon the soft interior. As the door opened, several reptilians grabbing him carried his limp lifeless body away. Michael looked transparent. It was as if his very life had been taken. Laying him on a slate black table next to the large egg-shaped machine. They replaced the sechuim device into his ear and covered him with a blanket. Michael opened his eyes slowly. His eyes were blue eye and fully dilated. Michael was completely disorientated. The slow whisper came through broken breath, "What have you done?"

"You are alive; did I not tell you that you would be?" Responded Nergal. "The amount of material you possessed was more than all material we have ever obtained from the Nephilim."

Clasping his hands before turning away he continued. "Very fruitful indeed…take him to a healing bath. Oh, and Mr. Michael, your body will regenerate in time, you will be stronger than you already are, I do apologize for your present state."

Nergal walked away revealing himself as a master of deception. The silver tongued reptilian emerging as not the victim of chance, but an escaped once detained overlord sentenced to death. A trickster. Nergal now had the power necessary to carry out his revenge against the invaders and only he was willing to do whatever it took to enact vengeance.

Nergal remembered when in the beginning he always wanted to record his memories. He carried a device in which he spoke, he would be remembered and have his life file added to millions of others in the Halls of Ihm.

Speaking to himself, "Overseer record log 1.5241.01. One of a few born through royal lineage of the first Ihm, endowed with the ruler lifespan. The Iln of the House of Aln of the Carian. In time the voice for all, 1500 years he had lived. When they first arrived I was young and inexperienced in my ways. Province Overseer of the Moon only 700 years old. One of many throughout 1.89 million years of existence. When the Nephilim arrived it was at a time when Iln were just barely leaving the planet again. Sending exploration teams towards the sister planet Gia. The hope was there would colonies waiting. We were wrong, no one was left."

Becoming lost in the moment he grew silent and distant.

"Then we found Simud. There was life on Simud, the massive beasts that roamed its vast oceans visible from the air. Seeing them with my own eyes. To the mysterious Tiamat resting farther than we could travel. Our robotic observers shown forests of life. The resources available made the necessity to travel and the possible return on investment insatiable. The crowning achievement of my time, the establishment to the moon base which made all of this possible."

"They arrived in dark ships that resembled long trees of unknown origination. They were old, many times older than we. Sharing that their world had begun a cataclysmic orbit through the solar system.

That would occur in less than 200 cycles.

Giving us advanced knowledge on space flight the new process of our existence was to relocate to the planet Simud. Their Nephilim forced to relocate themselves to the fifth planet, as their planet would undergo a cataclysmic impact. Every 365 million years they would orbit the sun. Many times colliding with smaller solar debris or passing through a gas giant, but always surviving. Searching for something in this solar system. We found out they were genetic engineers. We exploited this knowledge to advance ourselves. The planet came, Nibiru colliding with Gia tearing away the surface. The moon a molten victim. Millions of years' worth of knowledge of species buried in the ash."

Walking into a living quarter, Nergal proceeds to pour himself a glass of purple slime. The slime pulled from a planet that resembled a fountain. "They provided us with an endless supply of matter. We in return utilized this material to create almost anything we desired. Relocating the entire population of Iln to Simud. A new beginning, but in time, the atmospheric pressure not dense enough to sustain long-term growth. We were trapped while watching the Nephilim begin withholding material and sending their machines to repair the planet Gia for themselves. I Nergal, first of Simud, record my history for the Hall of Ihm when we return."

Nergal paused in reflection. The Hall of Ihm was made of an impenetrable material constructed by ancient reptilian Iln. The material that the Nephilim had given the Seraphim was first used to contract a survivor colony should the Nephilim be deceitful in their dealings. It must be trapped within the Earth under the cooled magma. It was his job to return to his people. The people living in the Hall of Ihm, numbered in the tens of thousands with sustainability for several millennia.

This genetic material from Michael, the being that had appeared in the hive during his death sentence. Where had he come from, he claimed the future. Whatever he was, the fabric of his entire being, the code of creation was beyond comprehension.

Within days they could now master cloaking and transformation into any being becoming a chameleon, the true masters of deception or illusion. He could create a device that if he could destroy the planet Tiamat. He first had to convince Michael to place it with Kulkukan. He then would need to figure out how to get him there.

Nergal knew Michael must be preserved, his material an endless source of power. Perhaps Kulkukan and his people also contained this same supply of building material. Could it be true, the old ones alive? How could it be true? Yet this being Michael described as an ancient. Recalling the history but not clear he moved to a machine. Speaking into his recorder, "Please recount the history of Seraphim and first contact on Tiamat." Placing the recorder into the larger device he turned waiting.

"The history of Seraphim on Tiamat, the Ancients. Gia-0.0354.02. Seraphim encounter Ancient Giants on Tiamat. Seraphim displace Ancients who have ability to teleport as interdimensional beings and vanish from planet. Seraphim conquer Tiamat date 0.8642.01. Speculated the building blocks of Tiamat made from ancient origin of Carian. Record end."

Turning Nergal lifting hand to chin pondered the thought. "Could it be, an endless supply of power?"

In one fell swoop the possibility existed of gaining dominion over all three worlds, fulfilling the destiny of the Iln. He would become the greatest Iln of all. Still 3/4 of his life ahead of him in the future he would reign forever. How long he had longed to feel the sun again, to walk among the giant ones. Giant lizard cousins now roamed free on the broken planet, a planet quickly recovering. Better their than Simud or Carian.

If Tiamat, Simud, and Gia were secured, the work could begin on healing their home mother planet Carian. It was said that on Carian the Seraphim came into existence. The creations of the great Gia originated on this world. They gave Gia her title because of the rebirth of their species. Gia was the God of the Seraphim, the creator.

He had once visited the planet Carian. The ancient ruins. The abandoned world alone waiting for healing. Runaway greenhouse of a society that utilized false fuels only to have those elements turn on them.

Nergal began singing the song of the Carian... "House of Aln, where mother is our home. The great one Carian. Rebirth. Return. Overcome. Iln of the House of Aln, survivors of the breaking dawn. Rulers. Chosen Ones. Aln. Aln. Aln. Aln." Nergal was slowly beating his chest.

4

CHIYE TANKE

Michael felt he had slept for a lifetime. Rising on the bed, he was tired and lethargic. Waking felt difficult. He must be recovering from an anesthesia given while he was unconscious.

"What had happened?" He realized his body was covered in a black skintight suit that felt scaly and impenetrable. Reaching to his collar he was relieved it was simply a type of clothing, or fabric and not a new skin.

Stepping off the platform Michael looked at his hands and his feet. Leaning forward to view himself in a small mirror. He was clean, healthy, and felt recovered completely. Nergal had entered the room. Turning to face Nergal, "You, you tricked Me!"

"Relax soldier, you were given the option, there are more important things to discuss. Namely, you should see what we have already been able to do. The material you provided has revolutionized our species. I owe you a debt of gratitude."

"What do you mean? You have already used the DNA to do what?" Questioned Michael.

"For one, we have been able to alter our own genetic makeup. My shape shifting abilities have been enhanced. For another, we have successfully created a super soldier, the Guardian Revolutionary Aln, "GRA" for short, it is a organic synthetic life form. Stop crying because it hurt so much and come see your army."

Walking through the sleek metal hallways Michael noticed an immediate difference. They were changing everything in such a short period of time. The true masters of building. Rising from a platform appeared a thin, tall metallic colored, Gray alien with large black eyes.

"That is a gray alien, a Nephilim?" Michael questioned to Nergal. "No, this is the Guardian Revolutionary Aln, the new sentinels of the future are emotionless beings that only act.

They will traverse the skies in our place. New servants. Constructed using the last remaining genetic material provided by the Nephilim and your own. A unified creation of your and the Nephilim species. The GRA pronounced Gray."

Michael responding curious about the progression since he had been gone. "I know these as the Gray as well and they almost killed me once, so you're saying this is something you created?" The Gray looking crisp and new, not like the old decrepit evil Grays he knew in the future, these Grays were off the assembly line still smelling of the packaging.

"Of course, I mean, you are actually the creator Michael. Without you none of this would be possible. We can create anything you can imagine. The Gray life forms are constructed to obey us; it is programmed into their genetic code. They are also programmed to combat the Nephilim, to expose them and infiltrate their society. We are arranging for a raid on Tiamat, to place several Gray's within their systems. They will provide access to a bio-dome. Could you recognize the bio-dome you say provides access to Kulkukan?"

"I think he would recognize me before I do him, I think getting into any bio-dome with the peaceful tribes would be the best first start. He would find me."

"You will take this." Nergal handing Michael a black smooth toothpick. "This is the chaos code. You will inject this into the core of the planet, only if you persuade Kulkukan to take you back to the core. When it comes in contact it will absorb into the core. It will blow the planet up."

"Blow it up? What about all the other people, the bio-domes of life? Kulkukan and the Elders?"

"The detonation will take 24-hours, in the meantime the Gray's will be high jacking one of the bio-domes to escape the planet, if you can persuade them to allow you that's one thing."

"High jacking a bio-dome?" Responded Michael confused.

"They are escape pods; it's how they plan on reintroducing life onto the planet Gia. Each is attached to the planet and one of their many machines. They are all detachable. If you can gather those you need into one of the pods, one could escape before the planet detonates. Killing the Nephilim. They create things. They destroy things. The Nephilim look at Gia as a life form, and we are all parasites who must be isolated, contained, or destroyed. Not after this, after this we take what is ours."

Nergal moved quickly as Michael followed through dark metallic halls. The material coating the former cave walls. Entering an elevator, they began rising. "How long was I out? How could you have done all of this so quickly?" Questioned Michael.

"You have been in a coma for 6-weeks. We have done this in 6-weeks. Like I said, we are masters of building. We maximize our effort."

Rising in the distance black saucers hung in hangers, thousands of in formations boarding the flying crafts.

Michael thinking to himself, Nergal built an entire army, the Grays. I thought the Celestials built the Grays. Obviously the Reptilian Seraphim are the creators. The answers to his questions were still hazy.

This must be how the Grey was defeated and to think, they used him to create them. But who are the Greys, they must have limited Nergal from creating for a reason.

"So what's the plan?" Questioning Michael to Nergal.

"We prepare for attack. We will take you in under the cover of darkness. You get in and leave the rest to us."

Nothing felt easy working with Nergal. He seemed so selfish. Able to manipulate the atom with ease. Power in the wrong hands could produce cataclysmic consequences. Michael needed to get to Kulkukan and see what the old man had to say, could he even find him?

"Once the detonation sequence begins all bio-domes will begin a countdown procedure for evacuation. There is no way the Nephilim can win once we destroy this base.

Turning he handed a black helmet to Michael, and walked through the wall of one of the flying saucers. Michael followed walking through the metal exterior.

"It's your fabric, every ship obeys its command. Your suit is programmed that all ships will grant you access. No suit no access. Let's take a flight."

Rising into the air, the ship shot up covering the distance from the surface to 30000 feet in less than a second. "We have solved the speed issue.

"The free energy utilized to make these ships operate on gravity waves. The synthetic DNA lined in the fabric in your suit, it is alive and programmed to respond to your thoughts. You are linked to the ship as well through this process."

Entering the atmosphere, Michael could now see the planet below. It was Mars. With the large Olympus Mons, covered in snow with trees, clouds, and large oceans on the surface. Large dinosaurs that resembled Brachiosaurus roamed the marshy wet surface. Also visible was a large part of the landscape barren, red, and dry. He could see the planet was changing but that would happen a long time into the future.

"Can we go see the Earth?" Questioned Michael.

"I was thinking the same thing. Let's bring along a few Grays for protection." spoke Nergal

Gray's walked through the wall wearing the same material. It seemed that the material that formed the ship opened to allow anyone with a uniform to walk through it. In an instant the ship piercing through space.

The feeling was fast, and instant. Before he could complete the thought process they had arrived at a planet with the lower quarter red with fire. It was Earth. Visible on the northern hemisphere was solid ground. Moving close the ship displayed mountains with trees.

Covering the surface spider like creatures, "Those are cleaners! I saw them on Tiamat, they must be cleaning the radioactive material up." In the air large diamond shaped pink satellites blinked. "It must be a security net; it surrounds the planet."

"I am thinking it controls the machines." Responded Michael. "Obviously what they are doing is working. This type of repair should not have happened for thousands of years, you said the two planet's collided what 400 years ago?"

"We could survive on the surface, they lied!" Nergal quipped sternly. The ship speeding away back towards Mars. "We must act now."

Nergal, leader of the oppressed. Knowing that this was going to be more difficult than he could ever imagine. He was confident the gallivant through space would have caught their attention. He failed to share with Michael that he was going to be sold as bait. The trap had been set.

Michael could tell something was wrong. Nergal in a rush with nowhere to go. He must be double crossed. At that point beams of light appeared in the main room as tall insect like grey beings stood towering over Nergal. Scurrying around the room clouds of smoke and moving mass.

"I wish to make a trade," … It was the Nephilim greys.

"I can give you Kulkukan" spoke Nergal.

In an instant towering over him. Michael watching from the shadows. The creatures almost ghostly in movement. Inter-dimensional beings.

"Speak" Thundered one of the dark beings.

"Not so fast, I want a guarantee." Replied Nergal hesitant.

"Speak" Repeated the being.

"I want Gia." Nergal spoke slowly.

Not responding the dark being turned, appearing out of the shadows the robotic Gray aliens charged upon the Nephilim. Gray beings overwhelming the dark beast shredding them to pieces. Michael was amazed that they died so easily.

"I thought they would be more difficult?" questioned Michael emerging from the shadow. Nergal staring at a pile of black powder on the floor. "They did not die. The master illusionists. They know I am coming."

"You could have gotten yourself killed." Questioned Michael.

Nergal ignored the comment. Gray beings began scraping up the black powder, putting it into vials. "What are they doing with that?" Asked Michael.

"More building material to create the ultimate weapon."

"You mean, the ultimate being?"

Hovering in the air the many ships drifting in space. They were fading in and out of our dimension. "What is wrong with their ships?"

"They are ethereal. They travel within space-time. Their matter exists here but supersedes our dimension. Yet, they seem trapped. This group separated from the large home world. Let's hope that demon planet does not return."

The Nephilim, resembling old decrepit Grey beings with bug-like jaws, praying mantis in appearance, long shiny black arms and legs. Moving in an angelic way like ghosts appearing and disappearing. The large black grey eyes protruding into their large twisted skulls. These were ancient beings, and dangerous.

"What do you know about these beings Nergal?"

"I know they are very powerful. They are builders."

"But why do they build? Questioned Michael.

"Why does a clock maker make a clock? How can he visualize within his mind the inner workings, the gyro, gadgets, and thingamabobs? Spinning, turning, and manifesting a master of space. They are clock makers."

Nergal pondered off as he continued speaking,

"When they appeared, it was for our survival. We were unaware of a cataclysmic collision. We had known of them; they had come in our species past. They are awaiting the return of their planet but its drifting. They are preparing life for the new Earth. It only brought captivity. I know very little as even their origins are mysterious."

While disposing of the ancients they did not notice emerging from the fifth planet a cloud of darkness that contained an infinite number of ships. With a massive vortex opening up with more emerging.

"Now is the time, Michael, you will go while they are coming here." Rushing to a loading dock Michael could see a black ship that reflected the stars on its surface. "This one they will not detect. It is programmed to take you to the surface. You must destroy the planet."

"Destroy the planet, seriously?" Michael questioned how Nergal had told him to just find a way to destabilize a planet enough to destroy it.

The collision of Nibiru and Earth wasn't enough to destroy a planet. Here was Tiamat, many times larger than Earth and he was simply supposed to land, hey here I am, and the planet goes boom?

The tiny black toothpick. Walking through the exterior, sitting in the soft chair, the ship closing over him and shooting into the stars, Michael was discouraged.

The lights of space shooting overhead numbed the confusion. Lying in a coffin piercing through the heavens, the blues, greens, and brilliantly lit stars illuminated the darkness. Cloaked the ship began vibrating as the turbulence of broken clouds rumbled beneath his feet.

Michael was penetrating the atmosphere. In a loud bang crashing all around him the ship sliced through the glass dome like a needle penetrating an apple. Coming to a stop embedded in green grass. The ship immediately dissolving into the back of Michael as a small spine.

"This technology is awesome; I hope I can figure out how to make it work again." Michael exclaimed.

Running towards the trees he could hear ships coming through the air to inspect the loud sound in the dome.

They entered through the dome unnoticed. Since the ship was retracted, no evidence that it was anything more than a meteor would be found. This was good for Michael. He needed to get away. Now he would just need to wait until they found him.

Finding encampment in the hollow of a tree, it was as if he had never left. The de ja vu of the moment. "I get myself into a lot of trouble." Michael mumbles to himself.

Red lights blinking on his chest. Michael rises to see large sasquatch standing around him in the tree hollow. Grabbing him by the arms two large beings lift him up, carrying him out onto an elevator.

"I am so glad to see you guys!" spoke Michael, thinking all was calm now that he was undercover. Their appearance agitated, edgy, and a bit angry.

Under the ground red infrared lights blinked in the darkness. The alarms of light emitted throughout the core of the planetary corridors that traversed from canyon to canyon. It was a state of emergency. Michael forcibly taken to the central hut of the village, no doubt to meet with Kulkukan.

Drug through the doors and throw onto the floor, he stood before the native leader. "Kulkukan, I do not know what is happening." Michael coming face to face with an angry leader.

"They tracked you here. You were used as a Trojan horse. No doubt they will gain access through the magma core in time." Spoke Kulkukan unnerved and for the first time panicking.

"Why have you come back?" Questioned Kulkukan.

"We have to leave. You have to leave now. They are going to destroy the planet. The Seraphim and the Nephilim are now at war. They are coming."

The burning almost unbearable as the needle like object Nergal had given him burned a hole through his garment. The detonator falling to the floor. Glowing bright red it elevated and pierced into the central core of the planet.

Violent shaking as the ball immediately glowed bright red wobbling out of rhythm. "What have you done!" The Chief in

dismay as rock began falling from the outer walls of the core of the planet.

"I didn't know" Michael responded. "It becomes my duty to destroy this world." Kulkukan spoke, Michael, thinking to himself, if Kulkukan is willing to self-destruct the planet himself, then why I was given the information chip to merge with the core, surely not to destroy the planet.

"Kulkukan, they gave me this chip. Said to merge it with the core, which it did on its own without my help. That it would destroy the planet", questioned Michael

"We must escape." Michael shouting to Kulkukan.

In an instant the ball stopped spinning as spider web like fibers shot out in all directions. The inside of the heart of the planet turning into a solid metallic structure. It is being reprogrammed. It did not destroy the core; it's using the energy of the core to build. The Seraphim had tricked him.

"Those fools, they sought to harness its power. There is an escape, a ship, created to preserve all life on this planet, like an ark, in the event something would destroy the surface. It was created to be a seed as a last option." Kulkukan explained it was time to flee.

Michael realizing the shaking was in fact tremors from the interior changing into a programmed building. There never was escape for him. He had been used by Nergal to entrap Kulkukan. He had sold him out. To what? His Gods? The dark benevolent deities who preferred darkness to light? The master builders shrouded in mystery and yet the ancestors to any biological Grey alien he was aware.

He imagined how it went down. Nergal convincing him to destroy the planet and save Kulkukan. Conspiring with the Nephilim to abandon the planet removing any possibility for escape and the death of all opposition. He did it out of leverage.

Walking to the central spinning core of the planet. The small frail old man stretched his hands in front of him, palms up. The tips of his fingers touching the sphere. Slowly waves of energy began forming around his hands. Glowing orbs of heat moving around his body.

The core glowing fluorescent green and emerging a green crystal shard. "Now we have the core power" Kulkukan moved towards a back door.

"This will take us to the ship, we will seek refuge on Gia in the dark hemisphere of the planet. I had hoped we would not have to do this, what a loss." Spoke Kulkukan.

Michael wondered where Kulkukan and his elders were visitors from? "How can we avoid the Nephilim and the Seraphim?" Questioned Michael overwhelmed with doubt and frustration, there was not enough answers to the questions he still had.

He didn't even know what a Nephilim was yet, he had understood who the Seraphim might be they were Reptilians. The wild monkey men of Ares, hominid hybrids created in experiments for a working force. The Big Foot, an ancient tribe of hominid being that is from another universe, and the Native men, but who were these beings that resembled the Grey only more archaic and decrepit.

So much of this seemed like reasonable grasps on the history of Earths past, but this was beyond that. Millions of years in the past if not hundreds of millions of years. A steel building 1000 stories high untraceable after a million years, considering several 100 million years lay before him, it would be as if it never existed.

Even in the Earth's past there are buildings of Puma Punku, cut with such precision, arranged with perfect symmetry each stone block like a puzzle piecing together.

Modern technology could not duplicate. In time, all cultures, civilizations expire. But there were remnants of the future, the roots of the future, present in front of him.

"Michael, the escape ship is ready." The Old Man leading them into a long cigar shaped ship hidden in the rock. All had successfully evacuated to the ship. "This is one of theirs, we hid it here since the beginning in case we needed to abandon the planet."

The Old Man operating the ship with his mind. It seemed programmed to obey his commands and thoughts. The ship flying out into the atmosphere. Displaying on the screen a world filled with domes exploding off its surface. Rockets blasting at the base flying into the distance.

"Where are all of those going?" Questioned Michael.

"Gia." Responded Kulkukan.

The surface a massive network of metal sheets and electronic machines. It was as if the domes leaving was a planned event. As if Nergal timed the inner core movement at the very moment the domes were leaving. It would show mastery of deception.

The cloaked black cigar shaped ship flying towards the planet. Michael could see Mars with ships not fighting, but in gathering life from the surface of the planet. They were working together. It was true. He had been lied too.

The large dinosaurs that roamed its surface captured to take to the planet Gia, or Earth. The reptilians emerging from the center of the planet being loaded into ships.

He remembered the Earth when viewing it with Nergal. The burning part and the clouded portions, but he remembered the green mountains, the trees, and the pockets of life. The remaining ashes of a once powerful civilization. The planet regaining control and dominion.

"We are approaching the Earth." Spoke the Old Man.

Viewing 360 degrees on a screen appearing in the center of the command room. Imagery of the Earth, the video of thousands of domes entering the Earth's atmosphere and landing on the surface in all directions. Some landing in the dark hidden hemisphere. The long cigar shaped ships hovering over the planet monitoring the reintroduction of life.

"What are in all of those domes?" Questioned Michael.

"All with life. The light and the dark. The entire spectrum they have created."

"What the hell are you talking about? Light and dark, listen Old Man, Chief, you haven't been exactly forthright with knowledge and information. Who are the Nephilim and what are they doing to the planet with all those domes?"

Angry, blood boiling over, he was tired of watching the movie wind away, get to the point. "They are engineers. Genetic engineers. They build life and they control life."

"When my people arrived here from a dying solar system in a dying universe. We found this world uninhabited. The second world filled with Seraphim, who were destroying the world in a runaway greenhouse catastrophe. An industrialized people intent on self-destruction. Our presence affecting their atmosphere when our universe entered into this one with a sound wave. The third world covered in ice many miles in thickness. The Nephilim have been on the fourth world with domes covering the planet's surface. The Seraphim seeking access to leave the planet Simud. To live in a dome upon the surface. You see many overlapping questions and timelines. The Nephilim are continually quarantined by the Seraphim to protect everyone from their selfish ways."

"They captured many of my kind when they arrived. Using our genetic material, they created the many kinds of creations. Many of the captured Chiye Tanka and my people were placed alone upon the snowball world to suffer in bitter isolation. Where you find a Chiye Tanka, you find health in the ecosystem. In a way, their presence on Gia brought her back to life. The problem we saw when the Seraphim started creating alternate species of themselves. Carnivorous beasts with razor teeth. It was the first thing they did with the material given to them by the Nephilim. The Cannibals got loose on Simud but were contained by the Nephilim. There are domes filled with horrific creations. They do not destroy even toxic life, they manipulate it and reintroduce it into an ecosystem always looking for something new to emerge that they can further manipulate."

"This all incredible things, where I am from these beasts are called dinosaurs and they were all together on Earth." Michael was struggling to connect the dots of so many overlapping stories.

"Nonsense, if they have it has not happened yet. The planet was covered in ice when we arrived. The Nephilim changed the climate with introduction of new life. We were eventually overtaken as they focused on Simud."

"Do not be mistaken, these are not benevolent creatures who promote life. They promote new life for their own manipulation. If a life emerges that is so detrimental to all other life, they do not destroy it. They manipulate it to be more powerful, have greater abilities than before and plethora of life are spawned from one organism whether evil or good."

The Old Man then spoke. "The Nephilim world currently can't return. The Nephilim believe it will but its cycle orbit was changed and they lack the ingredients to provide its power. Trapped between the orbit of two sister stars. It should not come this way again."

"Where did it go?" Questioned Michael.

"One of its moons resides as a much smaller world than it once was, trapped in an orbit outside of the ability to come this way again. If you were to find this world. It would most likely be dying. If you found the moon and headed directly away from the sun outwards of that moon you would find Nibiru."

"The moon?" Questioned Michael.

"It would have a large heart shaped scar from where it collided with the moon of Gia. I believe that Nibiru is no more." The Old Man spoke with wisdom.

"How do you know these things Kulkukan?"

"We watched as it occurred. The remnants of Nibiru strung throughout the solar system infecting other planets with organic compounds. The massive destruction of all life on that strange world. Beings that survive in another wave length of ultraviolet light. The small collection that escaped to the fourth planet displacing my people."

"How the planet diminished in size as it was hurled outwards towards the dark red star hidden just outside this solar system. They have not regained contact. They say they are coming back. But all indication, the once thriven planet is dead."

"Those remaining, doing only what they know. Creating. We are going to go down to the surface. Find a habitable place to hide this ship and survive."

5

SELF-AWARENESS

Nergal's plan had worked perfectly. Michael had led them to the exact location of the ancient invaders. They were the end of the Carian. The detonator in place regardless of whether Michael put it in the core or not. Timed to coincide with the releasing of pods. The inner core of the planet now his own.

All pods released and heading towards Gia. The Nephilim oblivious to his plan or to Michael. First step would be to gain access to the planet. He would agree to finally enter into a dome. To be subject to the Nephilim. But only on the planet Tiamat. Hovering above the prize gem of a world, the devastation could be seen. Gia was regaining life in all forms, a survival of the fittest. Those that found a way out of the domes at advantage for dominion over those choosing to life inside. Then there were the beasts.

Cities abandoned. Oceans of magma on parts of the globe. Electrical storms coursing across nuclear deserts. Bolts of lightning hitting the ground like rain drops in a never ending downpour. There were calm parts of the broken world. These would be where the capsules would land. Each containing experiments of life as created by the Nephilim.

"Enjoying the view?" The ghostly creatures swirling around him speaking one sentence among six.

The sleeking drifting Nephilim, swaying left and right with waves of cloudy matter hanging off his back like a dark cloak. The ghost creature with large black eyes and menacing jaws.

Arms held in front like a praying mantis. "We gave you place once before. Betrayal. It won't be like that this time. We will leave some behind but a group will enter into a dome on Tiamat. You can do your experiments and enhancements on them."

"I will give you something grander still. An infinite genetic code."

The sounds of six voices sharing a single sentence was demonic in sound, "Infinite genetic code. Provide. Analysis."

"A being appeared here several weeks ago. I believe you had a run in with him in one of the domes on Tiamat. He says he is from the future. His genetic code contains more information than all code you have ever provided, combined. I will show you where he is. You will then make my people rulers over all life."

Handing a vile to the beings filled with purple liquid. They moved out of the ship.

The sentence repeating. "Great Scientist."

What they did not know? Nergal would be in the core of the planet. He himself would detonate the planet. He would free his people of the Nephilim.

Moving to Ares who had appeared with a dozen warriors. "I need you to go to the planet Gia, break open as many of the domes as you can. We need chaos on that world. You will bring it. Oh, and if you run into my friend Michael, please bring him to me unharmed."

Nergal knew the material would be focused on almost exclusively, the Nephilim preoccupied with new technology. Referencing some unknown great scientist. Who cared, the only great scientist Nergal cared about was the one that would place him as king of this solar system.

The riddance of the Nephilim once and for all.

ON PLANET EARTH

Ares and the dozen warriors with him decided the distance

between the spheres made commuting between them impossible. Choosing to fire cannons at the spheres they boarded stealth fighters.

Swooping down between the tall powerful clouds, the thick pressing atmosphere, the sounds of construction willed the air as pods slammed onto the surface. Birds, pterodactyls, larger dinosaurs moving between the broken spheres. The distances 15 km between each sphere.

Ares accompanying the new stealth gray aliens who were flying the ships. In between them robotic machines working to repair any damages on the domes.

Lightning rippling across the fractured atmosphere. The volatile shifting winds, and the fallout were dangers that threatened the security of the domes and those they enclosed.

Ares wanted to hit the ground. He felt honor serving his creator. The desire to die in combat worthy of remembrance. His people wanting to survive.

In the distance Ares could see the descending cigar-shaped ship. Penetrating into a dark valley the ship pressing into the granite of the mountain until dissolving to the interior.

"We go, there" Pointing towards where the ship vanished.

ON THE SHIP

Michael had understood this was Kulkukan mission, his ship, his agenda, but he would not stay confined. He knew he must venture and seek others. If he could find Ququmatz, they could get everyone working together.

Walking out of the cave created by the ship melting the stone. Michael could see the devastation for the first time. A large dome loomed behind the massive tropical trees. More domes seen descending in the distant skies.

Fires burning, loud smashes, bangs, and screams of wild animals of all variety filled the air. The ground shaking under the rhythmic barrage of descending bio-domes. Each its own Garden of Eden, a safe base for all those who would venture into the wilderness.

Is this how it began? The story of Adam and Eve, being innocent in a perfect sphere, monitored and watched. All needs provided. Michael could envision the scene. Then the breaking of the glass, the realization of access to another foreign environment. The separation of the self from the source.

It made perfect sense. After all, he was living the reality and the reality was right now. Moving slowly along the cliff face Michael could see descending below the tree line several small flight ships from

Nergal's air fleet.

Watching intently, he viewed several dark gray metallic smooth gray aliens accompany the primate man Ares towards the cavern in the cliffs.

"I have to warn them. Carrying a laser pistol, Michael moved slowly behind Nergal's followers. Instantly the thunderous crashing of a massive tyrannosaurus rex plowed through the group throwing Ares across the ground. Gray beings crushed instantly. The forty-foot beast ferociously tearing at the prey without hesitation. Ares crawling into the canopy. Michael moving slowly towards Ares.

The Grays mounting an attack against the beast. Climbing on its back tearing its scales off in rampant efforts to

make the giant lizard stop. Only to be tossed off and quickly shredded into pieces. The men of Ares fleeing into the woods, everything and everyone fleeing for survival into all directions.

Michael reaching forward placing his hand over Ares mouth, while hooking his arm behind his back. Ares could barely stand or hold resistance. Michael whispering, "Easy big guy, we have got to get some distance."

The two drifting into the solid blackness of the dense forest canopy. The sounds of waling from the lizard echoing through the canyon.

There would be dangers at every corner, not discounting any possible form of creation that is specifically built to kill. Here he had an injured Ares, who seemed hell bent on capturing or killing him. The present danger of savage beasts all stressed in a foreign environment. The blood shed that would begin that night would be awe inspiring.

Sounds of chaotic screaming of all kinds erupting through the air. Michael hidden under the ledge of a slit behind the forest canopy. The sound of robotic machines fighting with the life forms trying to put them back into their domes.

Ares opening his eyes, "hey you rock, how you are feeling" Michael trying to make light of the ape-man's injury. "Me, free, me, untie." The words labored.

Ares leaping to his feet. Staring at his hands. Sitting next to the small fire. "Why do you follow him like an animal?" Questioned Michael.

"Follow who?" Ares seemed oblivious to the thought he could be subconsciously serving another unjustly. "Nergal" Michael was sharp and direct. "Nergal, my creator. own me." Responded Ares. "No one owns you." responded Michael. "Ares, does the Earth own the tree because it is planted in its soil? Does the honeybee own the flower because it can take its pollen? Ares, however you were created, you are the master of your own destiny."

Ares stared in awe, easily lured in by fancy speaking. Ares admired Michael because he looked more advanced.

"In a way Ares, we are brothers. What is the location relative to a planet, a star system, a galaxy when viewed from the perspective of multiverses? A drop in a bucket. You could build a new life for your people here. On this world. You could have independence. Choose your own destiny."

Michael thought about Nergal, the self-serving individual who had survived through cataclysm on Earth, a remnant of the Carian from Venus who was now fighting for escape from the chains that bound him to Mars. "Yes Ares, destiny. A life that you decide."

"Destiny..." muttered Ares

Michael moving towards Ares reached out to hand him a small blade from his waste. It was manifest by the suit that he wore. Holding it high with a slashing motion. "Where I come from, Ares is a God of War. A great warrior. That could be you. You don't have to follow Nergal."

Ares had remembered being abducted by the dark beings. The tanks filling with water suspended in the air, he and his people experimented on in diverse ways. The nightmares. He had always feared returning to those tanks. Being separated from the protection of Nergal.

Ares lacked the ability to reason. He made calculations separate from emotion that often preserved his life. What he had in street smarts he lacked in intelligence and yet it was his courage and determination to live that would always ensure his survival. The demeaning species that suppressed them as unintelligent apes had brainwashed them into submission.

Failing to recognize the truth, Michael believed that all species vary with none more or less superior or important than the other. Some have greater leverage or access to information which became knowledge. This did not make them superior, it made them accountable. Just because the bird can eat the dragonfly does not mean the dragonfly lacks equal importance. There is not an active bird vs dragonfly world war organized to annihilate and affect all other life forms. Here again, the emergence of forces of control. Tin Gods seeking control over their patch of dirt.

Michael had scouted the perimeter prior to Ares awaking and knew following the conversation over reason they would need to leave.

"Ares, we are going over that ridge to the large dome. We need to find survivors. Do you know where your people may have gone if they survived?"

"They here already." Responded Ares, motioning to the trees as six large hominids stepped out of the shadows.

Michael marveled because he had just scouted that area, not a sign of any intruders. Stunned how many could be standing in broad daylight undetected. He felt safer having the extra eyes of Ares. Ares was displaying a show of trust. He didn't have to stay or listen and yet he did.

"Ares, you can decide to go back to the life worth of work and submission which will become your legacy to future generations. The real question, how do you wish to be remembered for eternity?"

Ares looking left and right at his half dozen followers moved to surround him. The group staring at Michael.

"We follow you." Ares spoke throwing his staff onto the ground. The other warriors doing the same.

"You won't follow me. You are your own leader. From now on, you make your own decisions. You are only accountable to them." Pointing to the others like Ares. "Please pick up your staffs. Tell me you have a ship of some kind, we have to get off this planet."

"Ship, ship." Nodding, he proceeded towards the clearing. "I think it would be best to get the hell out of here. The bride has arrived, the ballroom packed and the party just getting started."

Within the tree line a small ship. The group boarding the vessel leaving the surface of the planet. The vast scope of what was occurring was understood when viewed from above. Bio-domes covering the surface with many more still descending through the atmosphere covered the planet.

Across the surface the creatures that had escaped the crashed bio domes varied from unknown squid beings to bipedal people. There were also many dark beasts, the dragons, the lizards, the giant dragons and giant lizards.

No doubt havoc on the surface for all life stranded in a reality that demanded only one thing, survival. In that environment, there are no rules. Creatures asserting dominance in the controlled environment as the war over balance prematurely began. The engineers had been creating a never ending cycle of life in an effort to produce something they lacked. Filling a world with electronic components building spheres to encapsulate all the varying life forms as produced by the genetic engineers.

Everyone seeking refuge or freedom or vengeance. He had seen the large lizard; Michael was not sure whether it was from the domes or if the domes had landed into a prehistoric Jurassic park. Maybe both.

Michael thought of a song, "Reverend, REVEREND come quick. I met a man in the sticks. He wore a cigar on his lip. The Devil wears a suit and tie."

Ares directed the ship towards Mars. Moving at a slower rate there was time to adjust to the escape from the hostile world. Earth in chaos. Empty cities, technologies from advanced cultures in ashes as the surface teamed with experiments. Among them the native peoples of Kulkukan and the sasquatch natives.

The rings of the planets crust illuminating the darkness of space. The continental shelf raw and exposed as vast oceans covered and separated the continents. Life existing in every extreme across the surface.

Earth was not yet home.

Ares speaking in grunts and groans with his followers. Using hand signals and drawing with his finger. They were making a plan.

He had thought quite a bit about his old life in the old world. The Tin Gods. Imagining a world where bumble bees subjected the ants in forced slavery. Michael was a natural philosopher. If the tree punished the animal or swallowed the bird for landing on its limb. Nature had a balance. Society was structured around willful slavery.

"Authority without wisdom is like a heavy axe without an edge, fitter to bruise than polish." Anne Bradstreet

The ship arriving on the surface of Simud. Landing in one of the underground base openings. To Michaels surprise no one was present. It was deserted. Stepping out of the ship, Ares looked at Michael with bewilderment. The place was a ghost town.

When they were last passing Mars, this place was filled with bio-domes as well as ships of the Nephilim. The Seraphim were actively moving. Now they were all gone. Did they leave the planet?

The rock that had held them captive for so long. Was a deal struck to provide them access to the core of the planet? Unlimited power? They obviously were unaware the crystal chard he had been given by Kulkukan.

What would be the plans of that wise old man? Now rebuilding on the planet Earth. Living in advanced quarters of an Ancient ship in solid granite he will act as prophet and God to a displaced people. An ark in time.

Watching over the planet. Its diverse archaic beings and life forms both hostile and friendly. Ares and his men disappearing into the rock caverns. The wind swept dirt spinning in the air. The dripping of water from fountains. heard from great distances. The echoing of the howls of wind carrying the silence of everything else.

Michael looking at his revolver, the laser bullets, the unlimited clip that reanimates bullets by reprogramming atoms. Where had everyone gone?

Since atoms are present in all things, the weapon would always be loaded. This was one of the many devices the Seraphim produced with the building material they took from his DNA.

Using the program like a man would use wood or steel, molding it, shaping it, it wanted to be organized. The usefulness in benefitting the progress of the species.

A panicked and dismayed Ares returned through the canyon. His entire tribe gone. Vanished from the surface with the remaining Reptilians. They must have taken them to Tiamat or to the Earth.

Reloading the ships they set course for Tiamat. Being

Nergal's chief steward they would gain easy access to the surface if Nergal was in fact on the planet.

Michael's mind was always turning and twisting in thought. He questioned himself, the motives, the way and means it all had happened. Is the plight of the Earth in one of those large 15-mile-wide domes? Could one of them contain Adam and Eve emerging from safety into chaos of a lone and dreary world? Too many domes to make an assumption that it was not at least possible. If not true, wouldn't it be plausible to assume human beings who were withheld from knowledge from birth would be pliable tools in the hands of the more advanced beings who will always view the created as beneath them?

He imagined what it would be like in that reality. The same being instructing the man to name all the beast of the field, that in a lack of his presence all things were beneath his foot. A structure of subjection. Michael had seen the extreme of theology. If he could imagine it, he knew someone else must have done it.

The Celestials were ruling without remorse; he knew they would be coming soon to this timeline. He remembered the story of their discovery of this planet. Would he view the historic encounter first hand? Was this why he was sent back? He would return to Nergal. He would find a way to get the shard back to the central core. Kulkukan had told him that the reinsertion of the crystal would set a self-destruct mechanism.

"Ares." Showing him the green crystal, "We need to return this to Nergal. You will say I am dead on Earth. You give him this crystal. The crystal will cause an explosion, make sure you give yourself time to escape."

"My people?" Ares was concerned with the outcome of his own people.

"Go find your people, send them here, I will wait with them. The future of your people rely upon you getting this crystal to Nergal. Give the crystal to Nergal and save your people, if you don't you will lose your people."

"Man master's nature not by force, but by understanding." Jacob Bronowski

As Ares entered the airspace he was granted immediate access. A recognized member of Nergal's command he flew uncontested to the leader's location.

Nergal had been waiting in the heart of the planet. Utilizing the expanse of space within the planet. A vast improvement upon the place his people clung for life on Simud. His plan coming to fruition.

A skeleton crew still maintaining a small colony on Simud. With others now implanted on Gia. Agents of chaos. The light of day for the Seraphim was coming near.

The Nephilim believing him and all his people contained within a newly created bio dome. Many appearing to replace the released bio domes. The process beginning again with a new cycle of creation. The engineers more room to store their experiments.

The decision to release the bio domes was because of the material Nergal had provided them. A new agreement in place to allow the lizard man to survive in return for the ability to regain power.

Using Michael to get the chard to the core. Using the simultaneous release of domes to convince Kulkukan and Michael the planet was about to blow. Manipulating the Nephilim to gain access to the surface of the planet within a sphere. Then access to the core. All the while, the Nephilim working in a mad frenzy to create using all material they could obtain that he had given to them. The purpose was to find the material to allow them physical form once more and not a shift in between two dimensions.

Seeking the source code which will allow them the ability to regain their form. Rebuilding their broken empire. Reconnecting with outer command. Nergal was successful fulfilling their mission. A new beginning had come. He was sure the Nephilim would realize the material he gave them contained 98% pure data which he believed was what they were searching.

NEPHILIM APPLICATION

Placing the material in their power core the central processing unit of engineering began to glow. A glowing white liquid surrounding the room as sprinklers began spraying glowing mist down upon the six Nephilim scientists. Each working to place the gel from Nergal into the machine for examination.

The machine began glowing and spinning light through the room. The six Nephilim walking into the center of the room. Their images shifting like sand in the wind. Unable to gain form or physical manifestation. Standing still the beings began rising taller and became more solid to reveal massive 30-foot tall muscled humanoids with pitch black eyes. Black scaled uniform covering their bodies with blue skin. The giant beings making orders that echoed through their station in deep rumblings.

Beings entered the room emerging as tall humanoids. Grasping large swords and placing helmets onto their heads they began preparing for war. These creations were different. Many were previously the hunched over grey beings. The bulging biceps of massive muscled frames were covered in translucent grey skin with pitch black eyes. The massive hands working technology from a civilization billions of years old.

The frenetic energy of the beings moving their fingers as keys appeared in the air using the material dripping and covering the entire room. The material forced to command the architects who were moving among the masses working quickly. The result was beyond their best expectations.

The creations that were not intended to exist in the flesh finding the provision to enter the mortal sphere once more. Succeeding after eons of testing and experimentation. It was time to return to Nibiru. It was time to awaken the watchers.

6

MUTATION BY DESIGN

Nergal had returned to the Nephilim leaders. They had summoned his presence. Moving among the towering behemoths for men they were cover in blue skin with workers that resembled white overlords much the same as Michael but more militaristic. They were humanoid beings but not men. Seeking to provide an opportunity to the lizard.

In a deep thunderous voice one of the beings began speaking, "What is it that makes our cells different from one another? What makes them look and behave so differently? What is it that makes a muscle cell look different than a neuron? After all, we all carry the same DNA. You are a geneticist Nergal and have provided the Nephilim with a very important tool. For this we grant you knowledge. Its epigenetic instructions that tell each cell which genes to turn on and which genes to turn off. With the different genes in play these become different cells and the possibility of creation endless."

The main being speaking seemed to be a scientist of extreme

knowledge. No longer shifting black entities they had form and dimension with depth. The being continued speaking. "In the past this produced a power so great it provided one-man the ability to oppress all others. It is why we are here? It is why we have done the work we have done? I am sure you have asked yourself these questions Nergal. The genetic material you provided is eternal. It has a chromatin that allows instant and eternal access to change, modification, reorganization. For any creation. Much of the cells imprinting on the chromatin during the embryonic development. The epigenetic marks on the chromatin give us the access to determine any creations destiny. Something we did not have access to with the creations of this world. We are aware of a human that you have come into contact. We must capture him. The next step is to duplicate this being, this human, make duplicates to farm for their material. You will begin the genetic process."

"Keep in mind as you engineer using his material the epigenetic marks can be influenced by the environment. The environment of the planet we perform the very same procedure all transmits as chemical signals producing new species. You have only mastered the organization of atoms by way of command, with limitations. The greater creation is turning on and turning off the greatest beings of existence. We have been seeking to reconnect with our true selves. To reverse the effects of our punishment by the Brahma. The first great scientist of our origin."

Nergal processing the information rapidly formulating his own perspective of the perspective this being was sharing. "Your species Nergal can live beyond your greatest dreams. For tens of generations your epigenetic marks can be passed down in perfection. We can assist you. You in return can assist us in the development of these clones and the collection of the data. Until this time we have both been limited by inferior code making duplicates of duplicates simply degenerate versions of themselves with each generation. The results were varying lifeforms but on the molecular structure no new code to utilize."

Nergal put it together. They needed the material to stabilize themselves. Finding a way to restructure their genetic vibration to this dimension, the Nephilim were now their true selves.

"In the distance is the Nibiru, we will heal the home of the architects of this sphere of sound. There you will stay. Your people will remain on Simud, Tiamat, and Gia. You will begin your work immediately. You no longer are forbidden from expansion."

Nergal, knew they may be misleading him by purpose to keep him separated. With his group in smaller locations spread across three worlds it would be easier for the Nephilim to swoop down and dominate one by one. It was an illusion. Nergal wanted to keep the Nephilim from controlling his people and tracking his movements. Nergal knew he would never leave again.

The leader of the Nephilim began speaking again. "It is important all duplicates are developed within the Nibiru. To ensure the genetic structure will remain unmolested by the effects of space, time and energy. From this point forward you will refer to us as The Celestials. I am Mastema of Dharma."

Coming into view on the screen among the darkness of space a massive planet sized, structure appeared. A behemoth synthetic world floating through space.

"This is the Nibiru." The giant leader Mastema speaking as if relieved it was still there.

The interplanetary structure in constant construction with robotic ships repairing and building along the lower right portion. Much of the machine rebuilt and looking new after its collision with the Earth. Nergal was noticing the red tint of the local red dwarf star floating just out of the solar system. The infrared radiation refracting of the surface of the metal that covered the world. The clouds in space swirling around the world giving it an industrial look.

Nergal was gaining a greater respect and fear of the Nephilim. The ship had arrived. The giant being leaving the room as the ship attached through the artificial atmosphere into the mobile planet.

Nergal followed them inside through the corridor into the surface of the world. Inside the planet everything was black with obsidian resembling surfaces.

Cowering beneath the multitude of giants filling every corridor he was cautious of whether this would be a trap. Moving deeper into the machine Nergal noticed the floors on the ceiling and ground had gravity. The rounded walkways dark and pristine.

They came to a circular room with a capsule sitting in the center. The room black with smooth obsidian surface. The cigar shaped capsule large enough to hold them all. As Nergal entered the capsule it sealed. The capsule was completely transparent from the inside allowing Nergal to look in all directions. It rose up turning vertical and yet this movement had no effect on Nergal equilibrium. It then moved speeding rapidly deeper into the planet. Coming to a stop he could see a massive expanse. The dimly lit surfaces filled with more giants working feverishly. Moving canisters of the material provided by the Seraphim. They were preparing the Nibiru for something.

One of the blue Celestials stated after stopping and facing Nergal. "This will be your working area. Where you will eat, where you will sleep, where you will work. This entire block. Notice the corners of each room are signified with a color. You stay in this section which is large."

The light a faint red glow. The working area separated by transparent walls that had an off color to them that produced a crystal clear lens effect for any who may be watching. They would be watching his every move. His engineering recorded into their genetic machines. The future of what would be created, milk for their blood. Filtering the blood and extracting human antibodies.

Nergal speaking to the giant needed clarification. "One cell of even a replica of Michael's DNA produces an endless material to replicate. It never experiences entropy. The building blocks, untouched. At the sub atomic genetic level, we have the ability to do anything."

Mastema replying with delight in his eyes. "Duplicate the being. No eyes. No mouth. Fed by machine. Harvest the genetic material. We will provide you with further instructions for others that will be brought forth into mortality."

The menacing giants moving quickly as if each were a genius scientist who understood all of creation. Perhaps only genetic engineering. Nergal moving to begin the process of extracting the DNA to input into a machine they conveniently had available. It had been done before, it was by design. Producing a technological singularity. Nergal would use the machines to create more gray soldiers. He would fuse the ancient's genetic material with the human genetic material to produce a homo-superior God. The sentinels to the Nephilim and he could get away with it.

Nergal seeing the positive benefits of the enticing technology. Using to his benefit. Within weeks the large Nephilim pacing through the massive cylinders with thousands of corpses contained in incubation chambers. Tubes pushing nutrients and fluids through the body.

The neurological inputs of all connected to one rhythm. Born with no eyes and no mouth. The frontal cortex removed. No differentiation in gender. He would clone Michael by the millions. The retroviral DNA marking the human's creations changing them on a genetic level to immortal vessels. The bodies sustained in perfect harmony. Producing unlimited genetic material.

In time Nergal would produce these vessels as well as many others. Nergal then used the abundance of excess material from the clones to create foot soldiers. His variations of the organic gray machines ironically within the world of the original grey. The Sentinels resembling the Nephilim although ten foot in height with golden skin, and wings on their backs. A hybrid between human and Nephilim.

The orders came down from the overseers that Nergal would need to produce more of the sentinels. Nergal responding to the request. "We can produce one every cycle hour. Several cycles of the rotating planet equal to Earth day. Currently 400 per full cycle."

In his own chamber Nergal withholding from their attention his personal creation. A seraphim that could transform into any species it came into contact. A true chameleon with the ultimate camouflage capabilities. He had created several exact replicas of Michael. Unlike the clones created to be harvested vessels without thought or consciousness he had created male and female versions of living humans. With every genetic human marker intact. These were his personal insurance policy on the future of humanity. His ability to prepare using the technology of the Nephilim in case of destruction was invaluable. Keeping them in cryogenic containers the human clones were aquariums for a future time.

In other research locations he had created something even more dangerous. Intelligently designed human cattle. Mute bipedal humans that moved like chicken. Never making a sound as they had no mouth or eyes. The vessel that moved. Absorbing the nutrients needed from ultraviolet light. One of many genetic mutations Nergal had developed. In the process of his linking and searching gaining access to the electronic database of the ancients Nergal was able to learn several things about the ancients.

Recording in his transmitter he expressed surprise to learn that many cycles of life had occurred in the past upon Gia and his home

world as well as other planets in this star system. Life emerging
and exploring continuously. Cataclysms presenting scientists with
decisions on whether to allow extinction or step in altering the
future of life for that world. The Nephilim had served in all roles.
They had ruled a planet that they built into a traveling ship. A planet
destroying inter dimensional ship. Moving in the orbit of the star
that contained the location of a world that would provide material
to escape. He knew they had preserved energy moving in and nearly
lost all their lives simply to course the world into orbit around the
sun.

It was never intended for the world to collide with a planet. To
their horror the very planet they needed. The Nibiru constructed to
be a planet builder. To harness the ability to access pure energy from
thin air. How the process worked was unknown to Nergal but it was
provided to the Nephilim or at least this Mastema.

The Nephilim outcast trapped in this solar system as a 9th world.
Until now unable to leave or move the world as it was

trapped between the gravitational pull of the dark second star
and the sun.

The collision with Earth destroying much of the planet Nibiru.
The entire Nephilim species sent into disarray. Trying to access the
source of power trying to harness the genetic material of their own
creations confirming Nergal's suspicions that the Nephilim had
previous access to the exact DNA of the human Michael. They had
seen this being in the past or some like him.

Nergal was in greater control here on the structure Nibiru. The
planetary machine preparing to operate for the first time in millions
of years. The span of history so immense that Nergal felt insignificant
when realizing that his species appeared to the Nephilim as genetically
manipulated frontal cortex operating lizards. They respected them as
an industrialized species that had conquered a planet and as masters
of genome manipulation. While not considering them as equals
Nergal felt that the Nephilim respected that the seraphim were
survivors. Just like them.

The Seraphim, advanced lizards from the second planet from the
sun. The original rulers of this universe. A story so in depth it could
not be truly understood by reason. He remembered the history of
Lilith the mother of the Iln. In an effort to increase the temperature
of their atmosphere the seraphim created an unstable greenhouse

effect that went out of control leading to their own demise. It wasn't the Nephilim that had done it. Kulkukan and his people had caused the end to come.

Nergal had not realized that even his species was founded by a precursor species of colonizers. Those beings the fathers of the Carian had come from other dimensions before this place had ever been. It was where Aln came from as his species simply adapted to the changes of a dying universe. They were the children of a once great civilization that succumbed to its time. The inter-dimensional and multi-universal implications of this ideological rationalizing could lead someone to give up.

The Nephilim records speaking of their supreme leader. The master creator Brahma stripping the Nephilim of the ability to contribute technologically to the empire. Out casting them into this realm. The database recorded only faint details on the supreme leader and that the Nephilim were deathly afraid of his returning. Nergal realized that the Nephilim were not Gods but and older race outcast and fallen from its own society. Criminals to an entire cosmology.

Brahma had taken the Nephilim's ability to sustain a constant physical manifestation in the rhythm of the matter of the location in the universe. Hovering between multiple dimensions. Put on hold in time and trapping them within a singularity in space. Was it this singular being that had the Nephilim working to produce massive amounts of the material?

It made sense. They operated out of fear.

The massive planetary ship igniting as the genetic material entered the energy. The massive steel structure moving slowly towards the Earth. Having to create its own momentum would be a long and slow process of gaining speed. The power of the vessel not in its ability to be mobile. The ability to move an entire planet even if by a few thousand feet a second is a marvel that could provide a planets annihilation or survival. The benefit of space, the longer one travels the accumulation of speed increases in distance. At one point the planet would be traveling faster than hundreds of thousands of miles per second. Something unfathomable watching the planet begin its lethargic movement.

In a short time, under the direction of the dark giants lead scientist Nergal developed an even greater humanoid. He called them Titans. They were advanced beings made with the DNA string of the Nephilim, while adding key components at their direction from the DNA of the duplicates from Michael. An army of giants averaging half the height of their creators. The Titans were fearsome giants genetically engineered to be warriors for the Nephilim but intellectually scientist and engineers. Nergal feared this type of creation because of the time when independent autonomy would be demanded among themselves based upon their intellectual capacity to think for themselves.

Nergal determined to fulfill his mission, in time, preparing for the day the double cross would occur and he would seize his moment. He too was accumulating power.

After six months of genetic research for the Nephilim, reports arrived Nergal that the Earth was under quarantine. No species allowed to enter or exit.

The planet, a crown jewel in space. A naturally resting world that will not succumb to the effects of space over time. Its location ensuring the maximum success of all life. The Nephilim fighting for this world. The life on Gia's surface competing for its own survival. The large giant Titans enslaving all creations while the Nephilim departed to the planet's surface for the first time.

The winners were the Nephilim, at least momentarily. The new rulers of the planet under the direction of the Nephilim. The losers were all naturally existing life. The human species residing on the planet and those in hiding were all slaves. The domes broken down by the Titans for material to build the massive Nephilim civilization. The genetic industrialized military complex drove their decisions.

Megalithic buildings made from pure stone formed by organizing large slabs of pure granite covered the cities. Entire cities raised on Gia (Earth), Simud (Mars) and Tiamat (Pre-Ceres).

The architects raising an empire. Building a duplicate to their home world. They were preparing. The reptilian seraphim vanished under the surface into the core of Tiamat with the main body living in bio domes on Tiamat surface. Nergal had traded Gia for Tiamat and unbeknownst to the Nephilim would one day control the Nibiru. He had the Nephilim isolated with illusionary power.

The seraphim leader Nergal building a massive force in preparation for the day and the moment when he would seize power. Reclaiming the star system for his people.

7

STARTING POINT

Ares family was missing. The troubled hominid struggled with the concept of not knowing. The stress wearing on his face as thick bags circled under his eyes from constant obsessing.

Ares lacked the brainpower to fully rationalize the loss and could not seek organized solutions to his problems. He was consumed in rage.

Michael had spent months focusing on avoiding contact. Hiding in the shadows waiting for a moment to strike. He was concerned with the deterioration in the personality of Ares. "Ares, you need to relax. We can't control what is happening."

Ares responding somberly. He was despondent with hands hanging over his knees staring at the ground. "No hope without family."

Michael marveled that this advanced primate cared so deeply for interpersonal relationships. Michael admired Ares for the humanity that was within him.

"Ares, can I share something with you?"

"Yes." The lone word emitted by the zombie like Ares.

"I want you to view the stars in the sky, the worlds that you know as trees in a forest." Pointing to different stars Michael continued. "Each tree containing life. You come from a tree, I come from a tree and Nergal comes from a tree. In the same forest. Ares, does the existence of one tree in a forest mean it is better and of more worth than all other trees? They are all the same."

Ares stumbling to follow, "All tree, same forest."

"Yes, all trees are in the same forest. Because life exists on one tree does not mean life can't exist on another tree. Nor does it declare a tree is not a part of the forest. You do understand." Michael was expounding into areas that had long consumed his mind. Whatever information or understanding Ares would glean he deserved to hear it.

Getting excited with the positive feedback, Ares responds, "You say I part of tree in forest. Nergal on another tree in same forest?"

"Yes! You and me, we are from two different trees but from the same forest. We are life, and life exists throughout the forest on every tree. Some life becomes aware of other life as they move and migrate to another tree. Other life control groups of trees and all life on those trees, and call this their territory."

Ares hung on every word. His mind was igniting with understanding. As if by design to accept information and process it. "Still others are taken advantage of by those with more knowledge. Ares, the darkness, the lights, the worlds, these are trees in an enormous forest. Each of us, you and me, Nergal, we come from the same forest. Among the many forests it becomes a tree in a much larger ecosystem. It is never ending. It is our home. Ares, let me ask you a question. If a fire came into the forest and you became aware of it. If you saw the fire was going to burn a tree would you try to save the tree?"

Ares thought deeply about the question before responding, "Yes."

"Nice answer, in the forest of the darkness there are some who start the fire to kill all life on the tree. There are some who seek to control and hold in bondage. Others to imprison all life on all trees. Some simply want to destroy. Do you understand?"

Ares pausing to think, which is what Michael wanted him to do. Knowledge brings thought. Thought eliminates the need and propensity to act on impulse alone. The impulse control issues were the biggest obstacles for those without knowledge. To act or be acted upon but why to act was what mattered most. This demanded cognitive reasoning.

Ares began beating his chest acknowledging his understanding. "Nergal control my tree."

"Yes, Nergal is controlling your tree. There are others more powerful, more knowledgeable than Nergal. Please relax, we will find your family."

Michael knew that the play on ideas and logic could possibly spark autonomous thought in Ares. More than anything he just wanted Ares to relax.

The analogy hit home for Michael. He pontificated on the analysis as well breaking it down to gain learning for the experience and challenges that lie ahead. There are intelligences aware of the entire forest and others that planted the forest. Within their cosmology of creation there are those in the know and those who do not know.

Is this not the dilemma of life? The not unknown more prevalent than the known. The implications of a hypothesis which allowed the existence of other forests or other continents beyond space, time, dimension opened up Pandora's box for the possibility of the endless stairway to heaven.

If a planet were a tree. If a universe were a forest. What if the universe were simply a tree within a much larger forest? Multiple universes coalescing to form a much larger tree in a much grander expanse. What would change within the mind of a being if their view on reality allowed exponential possibilities or an equation that would bind all into one? With multiple and endless universes on that macro scale who controls the game? Michael wondered so much about such dynamics of possibility. Is it the force that provides the nutrients from the sun or the force that provides the nourishment from water? Could they be separated? Can you have one without the other and still produce vessels for consciousness? On and on the questions mounted. No matter where he looked he saw symmetry and order, organization on a complex level that demanded a divine designer. It was as if Michael were in a program. Or was there a hierarchal structure based on status of place in creation. What does this all mean?

He concluded the existence of extraterrestrial entities did not diminish the role of life in the universe or the role of a creator. Not anymore than the existence of a grasshopper on another continent diminishes the reality of the human family or a grasshopper on another continent.

The true question when seeing reality in such a way was then to question who this steward over the forest might be and what type of consciousness he might find. As the facade of technological knowledge based civilizations fades the reality sets in, we are not alone.

Michael thought about God. Was it the source, the creator, the old man or something else entirely? He believed the greatest humility by an advanced being, is the admonition that they are a part of something larger than themselves. The human God admitting to the mortal man the existence of intelligence consciousness greater than themselves. The machine of life wrapping around all life like an onion where all were equal for all were a part of one. If such a being did exist, if must originate from a source. The spark of consciousness that determined too self-replicate and view itself independently from a third party perspective. What other hypothesis could there be to explain a universe structured on laws of genetic engineering?

In this reality human beings are simply a manifestation of intelligence. Vessels for consciousness. The consciousness of a God. Each creator existing independently and yet in acknowledgement that there was a first supreme creation. The possibilities excited Michael to the degree he was able to better view the broken reality he existed. His mind was touched and instantly pulled outwards to a scale few in human existence could claim to have experienced. Man, created in the image of his creator. Isn't that how the story is recorded? The belief so many have about the history of man. The fact we exist proves the existence of plurality of god's indivisible under the one supreme god. Despondent he thought about the self-limiting philosophies of humanity. Struggling to accept an ordination that was rightfully theirs out of humility. The virtual manifestation of deity, with independent thought, free will, and a click away from divine. The age of man was of understanding who man was in the larger forest of life. For Michael many things once stumbling blocks were now coming together.

Michael had often wondered about man's place in the larger picture. If man could reach beyond the confines of his surroundings to connect with the divine. When the divine responds with free access to more intelligence. Intelligently designed to operate as a conduit for eternal energy which was his own consciousness.

Michael believed when a human was born it was more than a machine or biological anomaly. The possibility existed it could be the birth of a God. Perhaps this was why the genetic material contained within every human was so valuable. Humans contained all the ingredients for innumerable life. Wasn't it interesting this was what the sacred texts tried to convey. The worth of the soul in the eyes of a God. The manifestation of the source in this reality and it manifest in every level of the human condition and physiology. Perhaps this was what the Old Man was trying to explain to Michael or what the resurrected being himself tried to explain to humanity

When the beings arrived on Earth. When first contact was made, there was a global crisis of faith. Looking back with a new perspective provided only by greater knowledge Michael could see with new eyes and a new mind. The existence of the others does not diminish the reality of a central creator no more than the discovery of the new world erased the centralist philosophy. Native men worship the white men as Gods, because of their greater technology. With knowledge came understanding, with understanding violence due to manipulation of that leverage.

Behind the facade are simple creations struggling to survive in a cosmic forest teaming with life. The human cosmology expanding from center of the universe, to islands, to living on a continent, to the reality of multiple continents. To the reality of other planets. According to the Old Man, it is humans who are the perfect manifestation of the source material. The origin of all life structured for the human reality. For Michael this did not diminish the importance of other life, other creations, intelligences, or the role that humanity will play as good gardeners. Even in a good garden are intelligences that seek to destroy, to vanquish, and hijack.

It is the duty of man to be steward even if the gnat devours the entire garden. To gain a greater perspective. Michael drifting into pontification of thought processes about reality and their role in human history. He had met all the characters of this play knowing there were many more in existence. He knew regardless of their existence a greater plan was in work. A shifting in the human experience with knowledge to achieve the true human reality. The human reality was no more than the realization that man is an eternal vessel operating in a finite existence. The realization of life on other planets beyond the existence of life on Earth or in any part of the Universe is a calling card for the reality of a creator and not the proof of the lack of one.

Intergalactic racism was and will be the greatest inhibitor to humanities ultimate realization within a universe teaming with life. A universe of genetic engineering looking to humanity to be its servants the same as working in a vineyard. Humanity could be the tool that God would use to bring them closer to the source. The source being the creator of all things. What if it were all true? Michael questioned his own role in two alternate timelines, his actions, his purpose, it must be true.

Back to the present moment. What separated man from the Nephilim was intelligence or an understanding of the way

things are and have been? The lack of knowledge used as leverage rather than as an opportunity to grow together. Let's say for sake of argument, that he created fire. If he withheld the knowledge of that fire for leverage. Does this make him a God, or a manipulator, deceiver and charlatan?

The problem for Michael was the growth of the Nephilim. In a short time emerging as supreme overlords consuming the vastness between three worlds with ease. For how many millions of years did they hover in obscurity unable to progress, unable to participate in this universe. The genetic material naturally occurring in him. They were waiting for the story to continue. Within Michael's DNA the power they needed to live. Was this not leverage that Michael could hold over them? If he could if would not make him the God or diminish the reality of a God.

Overhearing his talking aloud Ares had entered the room addressing Michael. "Do I matter to God?" Michael took exception to such a question. How long had Ares been listening to him vent openly? "Of course you matter to the Creator. Ares, you, me and all others are like tree limbs growing from the same tree. How we choose to treat each other is what makes us different. It is what makes us matter. You have the choice to kill me now but you won't because you are using your free agency. Your ability to choose to preserve life. This is a Godly act. Not all are like this, and yet, should you decide to make that choice would it mean there is no Creator?"

Ares asked him another question seeking answers to his own questions. "I wonder about why I am in this life." Michael could see deep emotion sweep over Ares. "It matters not that you are here Ares. What matters is that you have the ability to affect others. To preserve and not destroy. All life comes from the same place making us all equal players in a game called life."

"Game called life? I don't understand." Ares was not keeping pace with Michael. "Ares, let's say you decided to chop down trees. You notice a tree you want to take is home to a family. If you take the tree the creatures lose their home. Do you take the tree or do you move on to an empty tree?"

Ares responding, "I wouldn't take the tree"

"Of course not. That's because within you is the source of light. A bit of humanity to preserve life when you have the option of ending it. What greater purpose than the superior choosing to serve." Ares pondering the thoughts of Michael. He was gaining a deeper respect for himself and his role as guardian to his forest family. The removal of Nergal as God was very difficult.

Michael and Ares had two options. Go to Kulkukan on Earth or face the masses of large humans covering the surface of the many worlds. Their massive building projects expanding at a rate that seemed incomprehensible. The Nephilim were masters of reality. The emergence of a civilization of giants with all other life under foot. The antithesis of a creator or a steward. They were the ones that burned the trees down. Cut them into planks and sucked everything up with their dominion.

Michael and Ares watched the surface of the planets covered in these new titan humans surrounding by armies of blind mouthless humans. Chained moving like cattle to harvesting facilities it was unbelievable. Within twelve months the Nephilim establishing an entire culture that redefined a solar system. Michael had not seen such ruthlessness by captors. Even the zealot hyper-theology of Origin was not so harsh and who is to say Kronos wasn't acting in that way for a reason. The giant Nephilim harbored on Tiamat. Forming an immediate conduit for action that affected the entire solar system.

The Nephilim made no efforts to leave the solar system. Content that this was the place they continued their research, genetic mutations and experiments on the cloned human subjects. No longer developing a vast array of life they were focused specifically on developing human hybrids to harvest their genetic material. In continual motion building the giants who harvested the planets to build massive cities on the surface. The main goal of harvesting the three planets resources to power a large circular object in space they called the Nibiru. Michael speculated they were seeking to build a gateway or portal.

8

PARADOX

The perspective of the world around him was survival. The bartering relationship among the beings that superseded his capacity to rationalize their point of view. Michael was frustrated with the knowledge of the future he possessed. Viewing the process in action before him the question really came down to two questions. Should he do nothing, as interference would prevent the future from unfolding as it should and his presence would alter an existing timeline?

Or did his presence demand his involvement and this action would allow the future to unfold as it should?

The imagery could be viewed from the dilemma of time travel. Being a human from the future understanding the spectrum of information because of access to information. Modern day advanced humans traveling back in time 500 years and confronting the culture of the day. Would they not view the foreigners as other world beings, Gods? Confronted with this reality such cases could occur on even one planet should an outside entity begin interacting with advanced technology.

The possibility existed of preventing the initial attack. Should Michael move forward seeking to become further involved in the story with interaction that may be all that is needed to subtly change the future forever. He thought of Ares, the being making the steps toward independence. Ares carried such a stoic name. The analogy of the forest impacting the advanced primate. He knew his decisions as a free thinker would alter the future of his own species. After all who would know the forest and life in the forest more than a primate? Ares was much more valuable.

Michael remembered during the last days on earth the markets of the world releasing genetically engineered fish into the grocery stores. They were bigger, better, and promoted this nourishment as an advancement for the species. The pattern was repeated across the board for the betterment of society. To provide justification for advancing the society as a whole itself. Why not extending the same philosophy to other beings such as primates?

Ares was a first of his kind with the future a blank slate. Everything he would accomplish would be the first. The generational impact of that moment of tremendous significance. Was this why Michael was sent back in time, to help Ares emergence as a leader. Ares understood space flight, he could learn quickly. While he struggled with speech and independent thought, these weaknesses were overshadowed by his ability to learn quickly. Neanderthal came to mind when the imagery displayed of whom they resembled to him from the future as he remembered it. Of course this entire prerequisite on the foundation this was in fact Earth's past. It could also be another paralleling timeline, if this case, it was an unknown crapshoot. Ultimately he chose to follow a timeline that this was the modern Earth's past understanding it gave him greater purpose and that psychological advantage was needed. It was called faith. The belief in something unseen and yet you know in your heart and mind it exists independent of anyone else.

Moving closer to the Earth it was clearly visible what was happening. Ships covering the skies with charred smoke from volcanic eruptions blanketed the atmosphere. The domes covering its surface. He wondered what lay beneath since they last left. He wondered if there were survivors, how much life had been lost. He needed to return to Kulkukan and learn what they were walking into before he or Ares got themselves killed.

Ares speaking, "Must evade approaching Nephilim ship in the distance." The ship dropping to move adjacent to the canopy line of the rain forest covered surface they were moving towards a large mountain. Below littering the rain forest were thousands of crashed domes. The burned surface around them as wild life dispersed through the ecosystem. Their ship landing on the forest floor. The two walking out into the empty landscape. The surface quiet. The carnage must have been done. The time for survival at hand. Nothing willing to be in the open. They were in the open.

Michael could see large cigar shaped ships hovering like specks in all distances. So many that holding his thumb up, they were separated by that distance however some farther away.

"We are here." Ares was feeling a bit nervous as well being in the open.

"We have to wait." Responded Michael himself unsure what to do. It is not like they have a door we could fly into to enter the ship. He remembered they led him through a long melted corridor from the ship to the entrance. At the time a hologram produced imagery hiding the entrance in the cliffs.

"Back onto the ship." Michael remembered where they had been. The ship rising and approaching a nearby cliff face. Hovering at the side of the large imposing mountain. The rock face rising and towering over them. The sun setting in the distance. The ship hovering motionless waiting for contact.

With a sudden jerk the ship was pulled forward. The motion repeated again and again. Ares and Michael startled jumped to see what was attached to the ship. Michael leaning against the glass portal trying to see what was pulling the ship towards the cliff face. He could see faintly against the darkness long cables extending through the stone pulling the ship into the surface of the cliff face.

Michael realized they were merely twenty feet from the entrance which was now considerable larger than before with large sasquatch working throughout the corridor. They were accompanied by colorfully dressed native men and women all working on the structure within the massive granite mountain. Michael could see buildings similar to Anasazi style buildings carved into the walls of the mountains he viewed long ago in his dreams. Were these the Anasazi of Earth's past or a precursor mother culture that all native originated?

Michael needed to speak to Kulkukan. They were greeted by several native men as Ares and Michael exited the ship. No words were spoken but the native men motioned him to follow them. Ares received stares from all sides. As he passed all stopped to view him. Ares was unique. He was muscled, dressed in a fine woven animal skin clothing without seem or zipper. He carried himself with utter personal confidence. Never backing down from any fight. While extremely loyal to Nergal he never acted weak in his presence. Even their relationship was one of mutual respect. Ares never submitting. Ares was his own man in a sense, and a leader.

Everything barely visible through the dimly lit room. The center of the corridor 100 feet apart with large circular fire pits producing the majority of the light. The smoldering glow also a constant source of warmth and light. The massive end of the cigar ship rising in the distance. The levels of lights protruding along the rounded surface showing it to be more of a rounded skyscraper than the elongated ship which extended vertically into the mountain. Approaching the ship Michael marveled at the monolithic stature of a building within a mountain filled with fire pits and cultures surviving. Doors opening, they entered the ship. The inside of the ship white and black. Clean, crisp, and modern. The corridors exited by elevators rising to the many floors. Emerging from an elevator they turned into a large central entrance to a leadership style hall. The circular end to the room. Another fire pit only larger than any before was emitting fake fire. It must operate as a simulation but releases heat. He remembered the portable fireplaces from Earth.

Ares reaching out his hands to the fire to feel the warmth bewildered that it did not burn his hand but emitted heat. Kulkukan rising from an Indian style position. The larger ancient giants leaving the room. They were now alone.

"Michael, you are back. I am so happy you are safe. And who is this that you bring here to this place of refuge?"

"This is Ares; he is my friend. He is trying to find his family and his people. He is also a leader."

"A leader?" Questioning Kulkukan as he paced slowly around Ares observing him.

"How did he come into existence?" Questioning the curious Kulkukan to Michael.

"He was created altering the DNA of another species." It was the most simple and respectful answer that Michael could use in the presence of Ares without offending him. Though he wondered if the lack of true consistent independent critical thinking would cause any problem.

"Why are you here soul?" Questioned the old man to Ares. Looking puzzled Ares eyes moving left and right in nervousness he reached for understanding to the question of the old man. Michael marveling that the old man understood Ares without a transmitter in his ear.

"I am here to protect my family. My Tree. My Forest." As he pointed to the ground with his index finger. Turning to look at Michael for assurances, Michael nodding in approval.

"You are here to protect your family. You miss them do you?" Kulkukan seeking to understand the depth of Ares and the character of his heart began to dig deeper.

"I miss them." Grief swept across Ares as he imagined his family. The pain of not knowing burning in his heart. "How does it feel inside here?" Kulkukan pointing to and pressing the large beings massively muscled chest over his heart. Tears could be seen building in Ares eyes. Michael paused in shock, watching the discussion. Ares slightly twisting at the shoulders to the left and right visibly shaken from the question before responding.

"Incomplete" Holding his hand over his heart, "broken", then turning towards the entrance opening to the Earth, "Must find them to be complete. My only purpose to live."

The old man turning to Michael, making eye contact "This is remarkable Michael. A remarkable turn of events." Raising his hands in front of him Kulkukan continued. "The first independently thinking being with emotional responses and compassion which has been genetically engineered. The Nephilim have not done it; the Seraphim have succeeded at something I have never before witnessed first-hand. Of course because you and I being here now it must have happened in the past or with you from the future. Ares is a genetically engineered advanced primate that has

cognitively made the decision to become something more, something autonomous to itself." Kulkukan speaking as Ares overheard every word motionless. "Michael he has earned memories through conscious decisions which are a reflection of morality."

"What is happening out there right now?" Michael asked

Kulkukan who redirecting his attention from Ares motioned to a device which shown the Earth in digital form in the Air where the fire had previously existed. "As you can see this planet is in chaos. Lifeforms of every kind and size dispersing into the foreign world forever changing its ecosystem. This planet has also become something else, a world with more variations of life present than any other place in space…that I know of."

The Old Man pointing to the planet. "The Nephilim have filled Gia, your Earth with all of their creations. They are here now as you can see building something. Something large. A tower to reach to the heavens. It is expected when completed to extend into the atmosphere as some form of central connection for something much larger.

"A landing dock? A tower to allow access to the surface without landing?" The Old Man did not know what they were used for but knew it was for their benefit only.

"There are new beings I have not seen before dominating the surface. The image of the transparent looking 15-foot-tall humanoid walking among advanced primates ruling over them."

"Miskwa!" Ares jumping forward towards the hologram moving through it grasping at the imagery. Pointing towards the imagery. "My people."

Kulkukan continued explaining what it was they were seeing. "These beings are being brought to the surface. They are using the advanced primate to mine the surface for Gold. They must be intending a journey of epic proportions into space. The gold is needed to travel through space. With this much gold they must be planning something big. They also have much more power than before but there is something I need you to see."

On the screen the imagery of the screen show what appeared to be a massive interplanetary machine moving through space. "This is coming. It is their Nibiru. Their home ship. Interplanetary object transformed into a weapon. We detected its entrance into the solar system. It is on its way. I believe this tower being constructed is to connect the planet Gia with this larger structure."

Ares began pacing the room staring at the object moving across the screen. The Old Man moving to stand in front of him as he turned to pace back to the holographic image. "We will get your family. But first we must see what is happening in your brain."

"Brain?" Questioning Ares.

"You." Pointing to Ares. "The Brain is you." Then motioning to his skull, "You are here."

Ares lifted his arm touching his scalp. "Give me your hand Ares." Requested Kulkukan. Grasping his right hand the Old Man continued. "If I were to remove your hand, would you cease to exist, would you die?" Ares looking down at his hand and back at Kulkukan responded. "I would not Die."

"Exactly son, you would still be you. The hand is not you. It is a tool given to you." Moving Ares hand to the side of his temple he repeated. "You are inside here."

Michael hearing the same conversation for the second time marveled at Kulkukan simple ways of teaching. He was utterly fascinated by Ares, more so than meeting the advanced human Michael.

"You do realize this being will one day fill the entire planet." Kulkukan saying in confidence to Michael. "What do you mean fill the planet?" Questioned Michael.

"Ares kind are best adapted at survival. From the forest, which cover this planet. These are the trees of Tiamat which were taken and placed on this world to bring it back. The Tanye Tanka domain but the first home of the Ahtna, the tailed old men."

Turning again to Ares. "Ares, I would like you to know something about you and your people. You have a family that you came from called the Ahtna. You are the Ahtna."

The imagery shown the planet Earth, Mars and Tiamat. Small points expanded larger to show worlds. Ares understanding the imagery as he had acquired the independent knowledge through first-hand experience of their existence.

"The Ahtna came from Tiamat. This is your home world. When it was overtaken by the Nephilim after their ship collided with Gia they over took the planet. They began relocating the forests to this planet in terra forming on a global scale to bring the third world back to life. Michael, this entire planet is structure for Ares culture to survive as his people navigate this reality for the first time. Like you Michael, this creation is good having come from the same production in this place in the space time continuum. Any other location in space would have produced a differing variation and outcome. You having provided the material to end thousands of years of captivity by the Seraphim at the hands of the Nephilim. The creation of the advanced primate. The unknowing inability of the Nephilim to operate without genetic code, limited for thousands of years, until you came. Your presence has brought a ripple that will be impacted through time. Even my own people who come from another Universe saw our world end and were carried on the sails of space and time to this universe. That ending a new beginning for our people, the transition from one generation to the next within the universe is natural entropy of life. Letting time take its course, on the grand perspective it's meaningless to avoid the inevitable."

The Old Man always making decisions to preserve life for the maximum amount of time. Michael saw the eternal wisdom in the old man's eyes. He always made decisions with big picture thinking. He was respected and wise.

"The people of Ares are currently under the control of the Nephilim's new army. The creation of merging advanced human genetics with Nephilim genetics. A creature without humanity and yet the power of Gods. You have already made a tremendous impact on this cosmology." Kulkukan words stung and Michael could not let them go.

"I had actually thought within myself about whether to get involved but I now know that questioning is no longer part of this story." Responded Michael, knowing he already knew it was true.

"I foresee a grander plan for you Michael" Spoke Kulkukan. "If their planetary ship reaches this point in space time, the future of the Great Mother will be in jeopardy. Go back to Tiamat. Detonate the inner core blowing up the planet as well as the Nibiru at minimum severely damaging it."

Turning to Ares, the old native man spoke again. "What we like to think of ourselves and what we really are rarely have much in common. Look here, this world is subjugated." The imagery again on the holograph shown the surface of a place on Earth. A cracked dome, carcasses of massive brontosaurus creatures laying on the ground in piles of pure death. Other creatures he had never seen littered the ground. Packs of giant Tyrannosaurus creatures roamed the forests. They were seen moving in massive packs looking for those still in hiding.

"Why are there so many of those? Was there more than one dome of them?" Questioned Michael to Kulkukan.

"No, this is the life that existed on Gia before the domes landed. The tyrant lizard created from the radiation in the atmosphere causing this species of Carian to grow and rapidly dominate the surface."

"We called those T-Rex where I am from." Responded Michael.

"This world is also filled with giant rodents. In excess of 300 pounds. They infest the surface of the forest. These were the primary food of the giant ones. The massive bugs and insects as well all victims of radiation will fill the forests so be careful if you hear or see a swarm. The tyrant lizard king over the eco system, until the domes arrived. Then the Nephilim and their Titans sought to rule uncontested. The lizard now with equal foe with superior technology and forethought. This creature's time as king of the planet has come to an end."

Massive tomatoes the size of a basketball seen on the screen, "If you come across large deciduous edible fruits, do not eat them, the radiation within them will kill you. This world is the future but it still carries a bite. You noticed on Tiamat the entire surface is covered in steal and metal plates with the exception of the interior of the carefully constructed domes. It was all taken to Tiamat. The world must go."

"Ares, are you ready to go save your family?" Spoke a concerned Michael ready to depart on another adventure. Ares was ready as well quickly responding. "We go now."

They said goodbye to the aged leader again moving through the inner sanctum to the Anasazi peoples of Kulkukan and the sasquatch elders of a distance universe. Barding their ship departing out of the cliff face entrance into space back towards the distant planet covered in electronic machines of death. They knew the fate of the future lay in their hands. The increasing presence of the Nephilim a tightening noose around their necks.

Michael questioned, "How will we destroy the core?" He remembered Kulkukan had told him. "You must place the green crystal into the core. It will absorb the crystal. This interaction will cause the sphere to release an explosion which should decimate the planets existence." Michael remembered those words. Reaching into his pocket he had completely forgotten he had it. Holding the green crystal into the air he looked through in before returning it to his pocket.

Ares was thinking about what had just happened. Before they had left Kulkukan had moved to a large display case, opening the display removing a large slate black sword. He had told Ares the weapon would be of great value to his destiny. "This will belong to you. It is created from the material which makes this ship. It is sub atomically superior to any known substance." Grasping it in his hands Ares felt its power. The massive being lifting the sword and tossing his large makeshift stone club to the ground. Technology to match his skill set. "Remember, you must touch the crystal to the core." The final reminder from Kulkukan.

The travel to Tiamat gave them time to reflect and process. Michael could remember the Anasazi creating large murals out of sand in the middle of square gardens along the main corridor. The imagery seemed to be a depiction of the events transpiring on the planet. The vibrant colors, the slow process of creating the image. These were a unique people worthy of consideration as an all-time galactic culture and civilization. Then there was the Earth filled with new creations and new masters. The many Nephilim ships and the buildings glowing against the sunlight. The burning of many fires still visible across the horizon of the forest. The sounds of screams again echoing through the jungle.

Michael looking over at Ares staring ahead into the darkness of space. "Your people are safe. They are in one of the structures on Earth. We will save them Ares." Ares looked him directly into the eye before responding. "My people are in pain. I must free them." His eyes becoming locked in supreme focus. The sword of his destiny. The Gada strapped to his back.

Michael gaining a moment of inspiration, subjugation brings bondage. Bondage leads to pain. Pain shatters the heart and cripples the mind. The process stripping one of hope. The illusion of grandeur not enough to fill the void that slavery brings when peoples and species are unequally yoked. The imbalance detrimental to the soul and yet also the greatest teacher bringing a power within the self not found in any other struggle or victory.

9

CLEAN SLATE

What does it mean to have a clean slate? To have the ability to reset and begin again? Not defined by past mistakes, fault, or failures. The greatest adversary to a clean slate is not your own mind or the demons that haunt the dark corridors of the soul. The journey to be more takes courage, takes time, and a willingness to take the hits. The being making the decision to begin again is already aware of the past. It is the past, which motivates, drives, inspires, and rules the relentless determination to overcome. It is called hope.

The true adversary to self-improvement, individual growth, and overcoming obstacles which were impassable barriers are other beings. Beings who say it cannot be done. You are too weak; you have not done it before. Cancers standing on the shore of life casting their lines into the river of life, fish hooks dragging the soul out of the fast moving stream onto the shore of despair. The true quest in life to find the ability to shut the adversaries to growth out of the mind. Self-doubt is crippling. It can be the most destructive force separate from adversarial individuals of all. Self-doubt causes hesitation. Second-guessing to the commitment already made and agreed to within the mind. A bifurcation of hope undermines itself.

In sports the long jump is the perfect example of how self-doubt limits the ability to reach potential. The competitor runs down the lane towards the board to propel themselves as far through the air as they can. The only limitations to a perfect jump are the board, speed and technique. How is technique acquired? Through success, failure, or a combination of both?

From the start to the last step there are many decisions that need to be made, adhered, and a commitment to follow

through. At any point self-doubt in any particular moment having a ripple effect to every future decision. The hours of counting steps to ensure the perfect stride for their physiological form. Taking the science out of the process, it is repetition; more repetition is done on the run-up than actual jumping.

There are lessons in life to learn from this concept, the idea of preparation. The ideology that more time is required in preparation than in soaring to reach maximum potential is true. If the competitor loses focus not increasing in the correct form building needed speed, too focused on counting steps, or forgets to go through the motions repeated hundreds if not thousands of times before can result in failure.

When failure occurs the mark invalidated. The effort, the time, the energy focused in preparation being made meaningless. In failure the meaningless jump improves technique. In that moment the competitor has two options. The first, to accept the mistakes and use the foul for experience or to give up and never try again.

In long jumping there are six jumps. The longest jump being the recorded distance. The ability to start again, the ability to begin again, to have the opportunity to try again are prerequisites required to be a successful long jumper.

Michael believed they were also the hallmarks of a successful life. If the opportunity to try again is taken away leaving the long jumper with only 1-attempt, it would create scenarios of hopelessness. The expectation of perfection too high, the potential for failure equal in comparison that many would choose to not begin rather than try. The opportunity to try again necessary to success. The restart allowing the pieces of preparation to fall together hitting the board perfectly all witness a moment in time. The jumper going airborne. Will they rise at the correct angle or be so focused on the run up and board that the jump is flat? The long jump is a scientifically demanding event. With all of the dynamics associated with the run-up there are likewise decisions that must be made in the jump itself. Will the competitor explode from the board, reach for the distance, tuck the legs to the chest, extend the legs for maximum impact, and will the competitor follow-through allowing momentum to pull the torso and arms past the legs now impacting the ground heel first vaulting the body forward? Flying through space and all he can think about is the long jump. Michael began laughing to himself. Drifting back into this perspective will the competitor land feet first choosing to stop momentum falling backwards recording the closest point to the board as the distance?

Michael marveled at the long jump, it was his favorite event growing up. Running down the board, jumping through the air, landing in the soft sand. The feeling of happiness in success. Each time it was always about inner determination and having another chance to start again. Not being defined by the failed 5-jumps but rather the 1-jump where everything came together. This was life and how life should be viewed. He did not understand how some could be so cruel that they project their own unwillingness to take another attempt that they seek to prevent others from even trying.

Imagine the long jumper scratching across the board. Realizing their attempt, all of the work was for nothing. The energy exerted utilized in the effort. The questioning about where it went wrong as the competitor walks the 100 feet back to their starting point. Along the way the decision to take another attempt their and theirs alone. Imagine in this scenario individuals standing along the way saying things like, you are such a failure, that jump was a failure, you know you're going to fail again, why even try? If this persisted to the very moment the competitor had to choose for themselves to start again in spite of the negativity. Would the competitor be better off or worse off than had those around them who used the previous failure as an opportunity to inspire, motivate, and encourage?

Coaches are vitally important to athletes, not because of the need to be controlled but the need to be inspired, when failure comes, to encourage. In this situation he was the coach for Ares and Ares was the inspiration for him. They were preparing for something larger than themselves. Along the way there are those seeking to destroy them, limit their potential and be the dream killers to life. They were travelling to the distant world Tiamat. A world foreign to his history. The third trip to the dreary broken planet. The sphere covered in technology, machinery that sucked dry its life.

Much of Tiamat transplanted to the battered Earth, giving the greatest sacrifice, its very life to save another world. It was a forced interplanetary sacrifice, but Michael felt if given a choice one world would freely sacrifice itself for another. The core broken the last time he had seen it with the manipulation of Nergal changing the inner of the planet into an organic grey building factory. Would Nergal still be within the world? How would he convince Nergal to take the shard, to place the shard into the core? His friend Ares in full beast mode only wanted to fight. The Arnold Swarzenegger built physique of Ares resembling Conan the Barbarian. Ares wielding the power of self-confidence, waxing strong with determination. Ares believed he could be a savior to his people. He believed he could be the one to protect them. He believed in autonomy. He believed he was more than what he had previously been, Michael knew that Ares knew, he could never go back to the way things were before he opened his eyes.

Entering the space of Tiamat, the planet had changed dramatically in just a few weeks. The surface again covered with new domes, the Nephilim machines working feverishly to build more to replace the ones ejected. Moving through the atmosphere towards the domes Michael could see the formerly empty metal sheets covering the surface filled with seraphim reptilians. The domes filled with reptilians and not the previous variations of life.

What had happened? Had Nergal taken over the planet? Michael was convinced that from what he had seen there never was a war between the Nephilim and the Seraphim. A deal must have been struck to allow the Nephilim the planet Earth and the Seraphim taking Tiamat. After all, the rehabilitation of the Earth was all the Nephilim truly worried about. Michael also imagined how it must have felt for Nergal to have power again after obtaining the building material, that for centuries trapped him on Mars. How Nergal wanted a position of power, to live on the oppressor's world was the ultimate coup. How tempting the offer to receive the needed material that the Nephilim would allow Nergal to take over the world creator. They must be desperate.

The potential always existed Nergal would one day fill the planet with domes and then launch them towards Earth in one massive invasion. Michael could see the strategy in this on Nergal's viewpoint, on the other hand, the wisdom of the ancient architects with the Nibiru moving towards the Earth must have known this device would allow them to further oppress if not destroy the Seraphim completely from existence. A game of interplanetary poker was underway. The only unknown outside factors that would either help or hinder either side's cause, what was the trump card? What decision would cripple both sides bringing in the house's hand to set the field of play level again?

Without the Tanye Tanke or the native humans to allowing access the question remained, how to get into the passageways to access the center of the planet? Michael turning to Ares asked the question. "Do you have any ideas? I mean, you have been here with Nergal, tell me, do you have any ideas?"

Ares was asked his opinion, the decision as his alone. Michael had respected him. Ares responded confidently. "On the side of the planet an entrance exists for Nergal, Nergal created underneath a dome."

"Thank God." Michael sighed in relief, the journey over vast distance worth something now that Ares somehow knew the access point into the planet. Dumb ape? Not worthy of recognition as a species that existed in time which made a direct impact? He did not think so. This was a consciousness equal to his own. Michael remembered how on Earth the assumption as made that all life other than human was inferior. The inability to accept that any other form of species of hominid could have had a resemblance of intelligence or a consciousness. It was sacrilegious to assume they developed societies, contributed culturally with significant moments on the planet without suggesting that it reflected poorly on modern man who themselves are only advanced humans to those who came before them. Michael was beginning to understand the bigotry and discrimination that was rampant on the Earth before it all began was wrong. The directed unequal emotions against any ancestor of the human family discovered suggested the devolution of the human species. An inferior species. An entire culture running from its own past, a past staring them in their face. A history which does not invalidate their own unique and extraordinary existence, hard work, commitment, and follow-through. The modern human believes they are the culmination of preparation of those before them. The historical timeline the run-way leading to the board for the long jump. At any moment in human history self-doubt, or outside intervention preventing the species from soaring off of the board of opportunity can end an entire culture. Advanced modern humans were the representation of the athlete soaring off of the board, leaving the Earth into space.

Even Michael was the culmination of centuries, thousands of years of others running down the runway so that he could soar. Perhaps this is the real meaning of life and why progress, while not perfection should be expected. No man can make it on their own. All previous decisions leading to this moment in time.

But where would humanity land? How would humanity land into the future? The thoughts of a song came to his mind. "If these wings could fly, let's go down into the moment, we are lost and found I just want to be by your side, if these wings could fly. For the rest of our lives."

How Michael wished he could be the one to resolve the pain within Ares, the troubles facing the life in this place. To be master of this moment.

Even a great tree requires preparation, work and time. The mission of all species, to run the board and soar. Those who capitalize, that are able to adapt, change, adjust, those who have the courage when failure arrives to start again are the species that will define generations, define a life.

Michael was determined he would never again view another species as inferior. Even the monkey deserves respect for its commitment to itself. Its earned consciousness which comes from the same source that Michael's originates. The strengths and weaknesses, the commitment to survival. No monkey ever quit surviving. Living their lives in a constant jumping motion, an entire existence based on trying again and again. Ares being something more, and even himself only separated by awareness and action. The ability to determine for oneself in the face of utter destruction at the hands of another to endure most important. Even the monkey can show empathy, it is prerequisite upon those with ability to assist those without. Saved only after all that you can do.

Michael determined this should be how species from other worlds should interact. The common goal should be to improve the standard of living for the population. To provide the basic necessities for happiness, shelter, food, and hope for all life forms. They should not overwhelm, restrict, or quarantine with unrighteous dominion.

The object of the interaction should be to assist in growth, helping a species help themselves. With the mindset that once one is gone the other can survive and repeat the process. The great inhibitor to species is the inability to relocate from a world pending destruction. Without the ability to avoid cataclysm which will always occur in the universe, it will always be as if they never existed. If you never existed, then what is your worth? Where is the enduring struggle necessary to experience success? Yet they exist. Others watching from the outer perimeters of the worlds of all life, some willing to help and others unwilling to act. No species should allow another which is striving to fall. Michael would not be the first. If the time came to impart this wisdom upon his friends, he would help.

If his own timeline was nothing more than wishful thinking, dreaming and hoping for a place which no longer exists he was content in the fact this was his place, his time, his purpose. Even if he lived it alone. While hope carries him with the belief that he could save his father, his mother, his sisters and brothers in the future with his own action he knew he couldn't even save himself. With his own sacrifice Michael understood that his life would have purpose regardless of the outcome. He would run his race. He would contribute what he could. The end result prerequisite upon the steps he takes proceeding the moment of actualization.

Ares was not his protector, he was Ares. Rounding through the much sparser surface, with many of the robots focused and condensed in isolated areas rebuilding domes. When the planet was covered it was filled with electronic machines transporting life. Now they were occupied with rebuilding.

The entrance to the core was almost hidden. Underneath one foundation could be seen an elevator shaft leading to the electronics below. As they entered the massive opening the scope of the underground base of Nergal's seraphim could be seen. The domes held in place by an ignition system.

This was how they released the domes from the planet. It was void of anything flammable with a massive rocket blasting system in place. It was the same as a missile silo. The walls charred from the many blasts of the ignition to release previous domes. At the bottom of this well large enough to allow a 30 foot by 30 foot flying ship to enter and maneuver was an engineering marvel. A holographic entrance revealed an entrance that led through several other holographic barriers. The ship emerged into the massive cavity of the center of the planet.

To Michael's surprise the cavity void of any life. Nothing was there but the grey spider web beams that stretched across the space. Leading to the central corridor all the once ornate wooden architecture gone. No trees, no greenery, it was as if someone had taken a pencil and rubbed graphite on everything. The rolling magma along the surface shining light upon an abandoned post was gone. The beams emitted light sporadically. It was an organized structure. Where had they gone? Why?

Walking without opposition to the center of the room that once housed Kulkukan and his people. Themselves the oldest known migrants to the planet. Entering the room, the two stood before the large core spinning in the air.

"Ares, we have to time this right. We need to ensure that the Nibiru is directly near the planet when it explodes." Ares responded "I will fly out. Watch for the Nibiru and call you when it is in position."

"Is there any form of communication device in the ship that we can speak to each other?" Asked Michael confused how Ares would reach him when the timing was right to detonate the planet. How then would he escape?

Ares responding to Michael. "I will be safe to exit and enter. Here is a transmitter from the vessel. I will contact you from the ship." Michael was pleased with Ares idea. "I will explore some more here while you are out there, let me know when you see the Nibiru coming in visibility. Only go about 100,000 miles from the planet. Far enough away to see them and enough time to get in here and get me."

"I will use the ship distance to time it right. I will not fail." Ares turned and boarded the ship. Ares then remerged with a transponder that resembled a coin. Speaking into his coin Michael could hear Ares voice. The coin covered in pencil tip sized honey combs and gold. Ares again boarded the ship and flew away leaving Michael alone. Michael knew he was putting tremendous trust in Ares. Trust that Ares would actually return. Trust that Ares would follow-through on is commitment. Trust in the moment. Moving through the abandoned facility Michael waited.

The large graphite colored building that used to resemble a wooden lodge stood in front of him. He had time and he was curious. Michael could see a door removed. The room behind Kulkukan personal quarters. He was compelled to explore after all it would be destroyed in the coming moments. Within the rocky covered walls, the graphite substance was not present. It seemed to be the one place protected from the technology of Nergal. Michael noticing a hand print on the wall that resembled petroglyphs. Carved deeply into the sandstone surface. Nothing else present in the small room. Michael had seen this before, only on Origin. But he knew that even they did not own the hand print. What was Kulkukan keeping within this place he wondered and questioned. Placing his right hand into the spot the surface pressed inwards with the wall locking around his hand at the wrist. His hand beyond the wrist trapped within the wall.

Red light emitting from a slight heating sensation. Immediately the wall opened allowing his hand to release revealing a television screen. While not a television screen in appearance is was clearly an advanced visual monitor of some kind. The screen showing imagery as if he were watching a movie.

The imagery of a large bubble floating through a sea of clear golden liquid, with millions of other bubbles surrounding it. This bubble shown red to identify it from the rest. In an instant the screen magnified to show the one bubble bouncing off of other bubbles without incident. Looking more closely Michael could see within every bubble, numberless galaxies. Mini-universes floating in a sea of something greater than themselves, clearly they were a part of the source where the old man resided.

The red tinted universal bubble then connected to another universal bubble as the two became enjoined swirling in chaos. The space between bubbling as the opposing integrity of the space contained bulged in and out between the two.

Zooming in further within the red tinted bubble could be seen one galaxy identifying a world. This world releasing millions of dandelion like ships from its surface to travel the vast distance towards the bulging occurring between the two universes. Michael marveled that this species had the ability to recognize, then monitor such an event. In an instant the bubble released overtaking the other. These beings overtaking the second bubble of galaxies pouring the entirety of its matter into the second bubble of galaxies. A big bang occurring combining the two separate universes into one in an instant.

The dandelion like ships riding the entrance of the material like a ship floats on the sea. Emerging within this universe from their own. The ships dispersing in all directions with some landing on the fifth planet Tiamat. A planet covered in tropical rainforest and monkeys. A true planet of the apes.

Michael now understood. The natives were not from this universe at all. They were from another universe. This device allowing Michael to peer from a grander perspective something that he knew few could grasp. An explanation of the appearance of matter from a big bang. The native man travelers from another space time, another independent universe. He thought to himself, these must occur naturally. In a sea as endless as could be imagined, the numberless universes constantly interacting with each other.

Always seeking answers, he wondered how it occurred from the vantage of viewing the sea which contained the endless universes, trillions and trillions in all directions. They were nomads from a destroyed and relocated star system. The native man was aware of things beyond he believed any being he had previously met. What type of species could understand a big bang and survive the ride of the wave which should properly be entitled, the big connection. The native universe overpowering this universe. Releasing all of its contents into the space expanding it instantly. What else did Kulkukan know that he was not sharing?

Perhaps this was why Kulkukan seemed unaffected by the chaos as if he knew he would survive. Obviously, with this ability they could. The screen then showing the native man standing next to the larger Tanye Tanke native beings. Arms extended the same as the Leonardo da Vinci's Vitruvian Man. The smaller native man shown to overlap the taller hairy man with the two becoming one. The screen then displayed a record that the native man came from the sasquatch man. This was why they called them their elders. This was his own motivation for respect towards Ares.

He understood better than any other the value of life. The importance of respecting ancestors. This was why he brought his own grandfathers with him.

Kulkukan was a great man who grasped the humility to respect an elder even if cognitively inferior. A society that did not run from its past, but embraced it. Honored it. Respected it. Held it with esteem and worth.

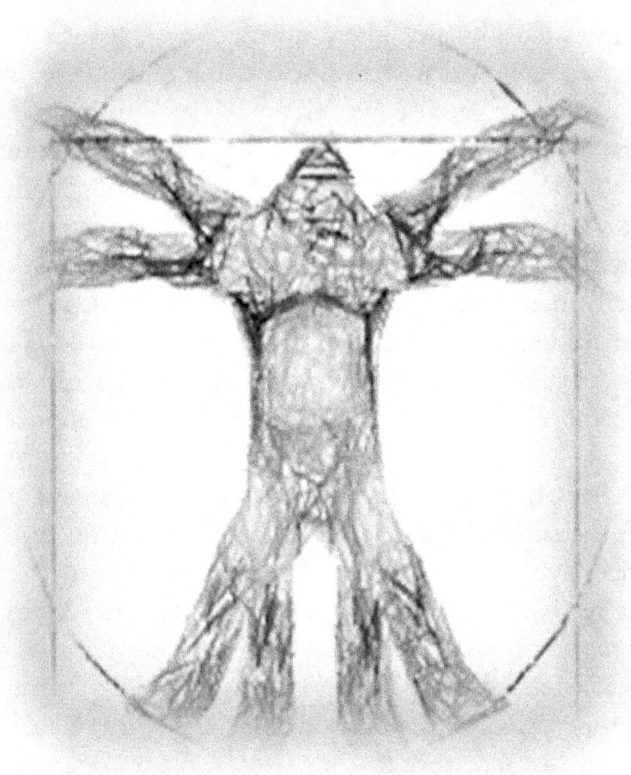

He imagined the source he had met with previously as the substance surrounding all the bubbles that contained universes. The controlled environments within the protection of the encompassing force of life. The ultimate intelligence that operated like a fiber optic cable enclosing all the bubbles within its substance. This source may be continually changing and evolving itself to provide for the expansion of knowledge from the endless creations that emerge. For Michael, this was something more than love. This was hope. The illusion of reality at any moment dissipating within the surrounding unseen forces that held it all together. He just kept asking himself with each revelation of thought, why are things the way they are within the universe of genetic engineering?

The screen then displaying a home planet in the Pleiades Star System. He now knew why he overheard many of the natives when he had first arrived her referring to him as Pleiades. He was the closest thing to their appearance, yet with lighter skin, he was confident they must have assumed he had come from the distant star system. It also informed him that there must be enough variations in skin tone that all native men were not native in appearance with many native's lighter skin colored in relation to their distance from a star. The organ of skin not the defining definition of what it meant to be Anasazi or Tanye Tanke. It confirmed to Michael genetic variation was by design. Space and time naturally producing variations among all species.

Kulkukan was their hidden leader. A leader sent to this place with the accompaniment of the higher order of elders. His mission to preserve the history of his ancestors. Michael thought his presence signified more. Imagining if the old man was clairvoyant of the future.

"Michael, it is Ares." The small voice device emanated echoing through the small room. Michael pressing down on the surface of the device. "I am here, what's up Ares? Do you see anything?"

Ares responded. "Nephilim arriving. Detonate the explosion. I am coming to get you now." Ares channel then went silent. Michael knew that what he had just viewed would be lost forever once the explosion occurred. It was his job to be the story teller. To explain a forgotten history. Lost to time as one planet dissolves into the darkness of space. Michael imagined what it must be like when a culture is erased from completely. Unable to save themselves. Removed from existence. This must be the greatest tragedy to a civilization. To be forgotten.

Michael would ensure they would not be forgotten. This story would be told and shared. He owed this to Kulkukan.

Seeing the seven sisters, Michael now knew this was either a parallel timeline or Earth's past. This confirmation meaning his action meant something. This was his chance to save humanity.

Michael moving to the central core. Lifting the translucent green crystal shard holding it to the surface of the sphere. His hand cupping the crystal. The dark sphere absorbing the crystal leaving his hand resting upon its surface. The ball beginning to crack. The cracking sounds heard as the solid structure holding it bound releasing into brittle powder. In an instant the surface crumbling to the floor revealing a smaller inner sphere spinning in the opposite direction. The sphere then beginning to pulsate long slow repetitions as red light emitted and then repeated.

Repeating as if beats to a song. The beats getting faster and faster. It was a countdown. The pulsations counting like seconds towards the final explosion.

It was now time for Michael to leave. Moving out of the central building Michael could see Ares approaching in the distance.

"It is done, we have to go, do not land, just move close enough I can climb on board." Michael speaking to Ares while pressing the small golden transmitter. The small craft swooping down hovering three feet off of the ground. Michael climbing into the opened hatch entering the ship as it turned to exit the interior of the planet.

Silence filled the room. Both men staring as if in hyper-focus to escape. The ship began moving through the corridor increasing speed, up the cylinder dome shaft, emerging into the atmosphere.

The imagery of the massive planet sized ship hovered like a moon just outside the atmosphere of the planet. The scope in size of this Nibiru creation too massive to describe. The Nibiru was a ship and it was formidable.

Michael redirected his attention to the mission. "Make way for Gia, Ares. We must get out of the direction of this explosion." Michael speaking with urgency in his tone.

He was worried. Ares and he may be too close to the explosion. He did not even know when it would occur. He only knew the massive spherical ship of the Nephilim moved slower than their small craft.

The reptilian on the surface and the Nephilim in the Nibiru unaware of the explosion that would occur. This was their moment. The heaving planet finally allowed to move on. For millions of years giving its life force for all who wished to take. Always giving the planet was a living organism. A living organism held alive by parasitic life forms subjugating it to life support. The metal framework holding it bound in permanent stasis. The hollowed out core giving way.

Michael felt a sense of moral obligation to free the dying world

Nibiru from the grasp of the Nephilim and the Seraphim. Even planets could live. Even the Nibiru was a world not allowed to transition. A planet held hostage by technology. A corpse floating through space. It was a new perspective to view a planet from this vantage. As a living being.

Michael felt no obligation to warn the reptilian on the surface. They were a selfish species. A species without empathy, without a conscience. Driven for personal gain, at the sacrifice of any and all. He also felt no sympathy for the grey Nephilim, the dark creatures, the precursors to the Grays. Michael did wonder how they connected to the future Greys who called themselves Celestials outcast from the Royal Ones of Origin.

These beings needed to be destroyed. To cut the head off the snake. To remove their ability to access any technology that would allow them continued enslavement of other races. The mad scientists who created life but also had no respect to the life they created and no moral obligation to ensure it was given a proper opportunity to survive. Sending all those pods to Earth, it was heartless, immediately leading many to extinction. Michael did not intend to be heartless but he knew, it was better a few should perish than generations.

The ship moving past Mars and towards the Earth. Tiamat drifting into the distance as a faint star. The ship coming to a rest behind the dark side of the moon. A moon itself a reconstruction with portions of it hollowed out. Even here they would need to remain in stealth. The reptilian with their Gray machines and the Grey's from which they were modeled. "Ares, are we able to zoom in and view the explosion from this vantage using this ships systems, is this possible?"

"Only with the visual enhancer." Ares started pushing controls. The screen shown the world. The final image of the planet. It was heart breaking what the Nephilim had done to its surface in the name of progress. The Nibiru moving by the planet 1/4th of its size enormous in proportions. In an instant Michael could see hundreds of ships launching form the surface of Tiamat. They were fleeing. How did they know?

He noticed the large Nibiru powering up as brilliantly lit light moved through the lines that formed its equatorial lines vertically and horizontally. The screen went bright white as the explosion of the planet occurred.

10

NIBIRU

Nergal had dreamt of reuniting with his people. Once the Nibiru reached Gia he would release his army of sentinels. He would seize control. The Nibiru now passing Jupiter. Nergal knew the fulfillment of his destiny was at hand. He would bring honor back to the Aln. The ship almost entirely under his control. A majority of the Nephilim living in ships hovering above the atmosphere of Gia. He was the master of the helm. His plan was working perfectly.

The Grey machines mixed among the Titans on Gia. The foot soldiers to ensure the dark leaders commands were met. It all hinged on Tiamat and the transaction with the Nephilim. They would give the planet to the Seraphim in return for a predetermined amount of source material. The only requirement, Nergal remain on the Nibiru. The Nephilim moving to phase III of their plan to organize a kingdom on the third planet.

Nergal knew, if he could destroy Gia, he could destroy the Nephilim. He would use the Nibiru to destroy Gia. Coming to the planet Tiamat Nergal's attention moved towards accessing his people once more. The savior arriving for a global victory. In the next breath red lights blinking on and off as the planet was scanned. A master voice sounding over the electrical equipment. "Planetary collapse imminent, central core collapse."

"NO!!" Nergal yelling through the room had the carpet of destiny ripped from beneath him.

The scan showing an image of the planet displaying the central core collapsing the inner cavity of the planet. The planet collapsing on itself producing an outward explosion that would reach the Nibiru. The computer of the ship again alerting Nergal to the coming cataclysm. "System, will the Nibiru survive the explosion?" "Interplanetary rupture imminent, Nibiru will be destroyed." The answer from the machine devastating.

Nergal quickly activated the escape ship command within the Nibiru. This would reach the Nephilim. "Nephilim, Tiamat destruction imminent. Interplanetary core collapse. Nibiru destruction expected. Seek refuge on Gia. Collapse imminent." Nergal ended the broadcast signal and fled towards the landing corridors. He knew in this moment none could keep him from escaping.

His army of soldiers loyal only to himself. Appearing from every corner to accompany their leader to safety. The grey machines producing a substance that organized into a capsule which shot Nergal into the darkness of space towards Gia. The grey machines themselves turning into saucer shaped ships. They were shape shifting Nano-bots. A new technology for the future as designed by Nergal. These Grays would revolutionize the future of the Seraphim. Thousands of these beings releasing into space fleeing the imminent destruction. The signal reaching the surface of Tiamat, the high leaders likewise releasing from the planet.

In an instant the planet collapsing to a point and then dispersing in a massive explosion. The explosion sending a title wave warp of space outwards. The planet breathing its final breath of life, emitting its life into space surrounded the Nibiru. The home of the Nephilim exploding the planet melting and twisting upon itself. Moving through space Nergal was horrified that his object of control was gone. His position of power removed. He was now a nomad on the planet Gia, beneath the Nephilim once more but he had removed a few pieces from the board or play. There was always a silver lining in defeat. This was something he could not bear. It could have gone any number of directions. He had placed the core in a stasis. It should never have ruptured.

The ripple of space moving towards Simud. The impact of the gravitational wave released by the massive planets destruction impacting the planet Simud with tremendous force. The ripping at the atmosphere of Mars. The electromagnetic field stretching as if it were being lifted from the planet. Viewing the damage from a safe location near Gia, Nergal watched as the computer system informed him of the status of the explosion.

"System analysis, Tiamat destroyed, Nibiru destroyed. Simud not destroyed, planetary body facing cataclysmic climate change with 70% of the atmosphere blown into space." The screen showed a detailed analysis of the planets electromagnetic field. The field ripping into space stretching like an elongated oval. "Current analysis, remaining 10% of atmospheric loss in next 3-planetary rotations."

The end for Simud was fast. The unseen gravitational wave removing the magnetic field which held the planet safe against the elements of space. In one moment a lush world of savannah grasslands surrounding large oceans. The next a barren landscape with oceans blasted into space. The icebergs traveling at super speeds in the direction of the Earth. The shell that contained the atmosphere had been removed. The atmosphere releasing into space as the planet experienced sudden and immediate shock. Nergal watched as the planets massive oceans began to be sucked into space freezing into massive chunks of ice debris. The surface instantly changing from lush green vegetation to death and destruction. The remaining atmosphere producing only ice as the oceans were pulled to the poles with the expanding and stretching magnetic field.

The life in the planet, those few who remained in the vast cities under the surface unknowingly trapped in a global cataclysm. The debris from Tiamat also reigning down upon its surface in massive explosions. The rubber band effect had occurred with a gravitational wave moving towards the earth. In 1-Earth hour Simud was no more.

The entire dynamic of the solar system changed, two of three habitable worlds eliminated. Once four life supporting planets now reduced only to Gia. The desperation of all species caught in the midst of a war in heaven. Nergal's primary focus to seek refuge in the planet Gia. To reevaluate their next move. Gia now the potluck of the solar system.

Without the Nibiru the Nephilim were crippled beyond repair. No longer interstellar, no longer interplanetary, they were nomads. All life upon the face of the planet were a collection of nomads. Nergal cringing at the day he would have to share anything with the Nephilim. Let alone a home world with innumerable surface and space dwellers peering down upon him.

"I will not share this planet." He said to himself. Choosing to land in the sparsest place of the planet Nergal and his army of greys and Seraphim landed at the South Pole. Establishing a beacon that only his kind could receive instructed those that fled Tiamat before its destruction to make way for refuge in the frozen South Pole of the planet. The temperature detrimental to his species. These were times of survival. No longer conquest. The dreams of self-actualizing the destiny of the Seraphim. Seraphim were the fathers of this universe.

Nergal was in possession of his insurance policy. The humanoid creations. The clones. The many Grey's utilizing the material to formulate an underground entrance and base within the ice as if cutting butter with a hot knife.

The speed in which the hundreds of gray machines operated was mesmerizing. Nergal entering a prepared room. The clear glass coffins containing the bodies still sealed. Nergal moving to one containing a woman, pressing several transparent keys the lid emitting steam as it slid open. The human being contained inside subject to the temperature of the planet. Nergal was bringing them to life.

There were eight beings both female to male. All in the image of Michael using his DNA as the basis for cloning. These Seraphim created humans would also serve to provide the needed material for Nergal to rebuild. This would be their rebirth and the day would come when they would one day rule the planet. Nergal knew within his mind, with 1200 Gia years remaining in his life span, his leadership and determination would be fundamentally required to restore their once great civilization.

Speaking aloud Nergal declared. "I will now become the King of the Sunset. As the sun rises from the East so shall the Seraphim rise to cover the expanse of this planet to remove all others from our kingdom." He moved to one of the clones. Speaking to the now breathing genetically engineered blond haired, blue eyed human Nergal continued. "You will have a great destiny. To create as much chaos and conflict amongst the societies of the surface. To assist in the reemergence of the race. My children, the merging of human with Seraphim. The turn their negative emotions towards our advantage. To inspire greed, hate, wrath, and envy. You will be our lifeblood as well. You are the Illuminati. The Seraphim's army on this planet."

Nergal knew that this was not the first time an illuminati had been created. The sacred Seraphim term for the elite guard. Created throughout time to be guardians, the eyes and the ears of the species. These were superior to anything before endeavored. The primates were hoped to fill this sacred role, to act as intermediaries between the rulers of the world and outside inhabitants. These were more, they contained power. He would fill the Earth with his creations. His humans. Working side by side his Grays' they would not be stopped. Nergal was not a quitter, he was an expert in outwitting the opposition.

One of the beings opening its eyes as Nergal rushed over speaking. "My son, rise." The human sat upwards in the stasis chamber, still taking in deep breathes. Staring confused at Nergal. "Can you understand me child?"

The being nodding. Retaining the basic cognitive functions of Michael, a residual of understanding remained. The process had worked. The man spoke, "Father?" Nergal responding with a stern voice. "Master." Then reaching forward touching the chest of the man. "You are Glycon."

Turning towards the others now rising from their stasis chambers they had been watching. "I am Nergal, your Master and you're Creator. This is Glycon, he will be King among you." One of the beings speaking for the first time, "Who am I?" Nergal moving towards them "You are my children. I will call you Lamia, and you Wadjet" the two females smiling in acceptance. Moving towards the remaining five humans touching them on the shoulder, "Naga, Shokera, Cecrops, Zahnak, and you are Nuwa." Lamia, Wadjet and Nuwa female with the remainder male. "My high council in the centuries to come among all cultures, peoples and races that will cover this planet."

As gray machines moved to place uniforms and clothing onto the humans. The uniforms were pure black in appearance made of small honeycombs, the suit the same material the grays were constructed from.

"Each one of you have been given gifts and abilities. You have within you a knowledge of this world. This was by design. Look down at your skin. It is able to adapt to any living organism." Reaching out to one of the Grays, Nergal pulled them close. "I want each of you to change to be in appearance as this being"

Looking down at their skin then back up at the gray being, their skin rippling like needles as it folded reversing to reflect the outside appearance of the grey. One by one they each shape shifted to resemble a gray being. "This will ensure your survival. You are illuminati. Always adapting, changing, shifting, you have been given superior enlightenment to the world you will confront."

"One day your descendants will populate the surface of this planet. On that day you will assist in allowing the Iln of the House of Aln of the once great Carian to once again regain power over the cosmos."

The eight humans shifting back to human form began moving towards the many machines. They retained all memory of Michael once born retaining a genetic memory. This genetic memory they were able to work faster than the many grays.

"I want you to shift to your true form, the Seraphim within you." Stepping forward he asked each of them to form a circle around him. With hands placed on Nergal, he began speaking again. "My children, repeat after me. This is the song of the Carian of the House of Aln"

He began the chant. "House of Aln, where mother is our home. The great one Carian. Rebirth. Return. Overcome. Iln of the House of Aln, survivors of the breaking Dawn. Rulers. Chosen Ones. Aln. Aln. Aln. Aln."

In that moment the humans looking at each other. Everyone were reptilian in appearance. "This is your true form. You are Iln of the House of Aln, the children of Carian. Never forget who you are, you are Seraphim. Your problem solving abilities will surpass even the Gray. Each of you will now enter the bio-shifter" Motioning to the same device that Michael had originally entered, one by one they entered and exited. Experiencing the same translucent skin color as Michael. They were vessels for harvesting. Genetically engineered beings with a living soul.

Nergal's contingency plan was always his best, while he would have liked to have everything flow smoothly and easily take the planet over. He also cherished the opportunity to freely build his own planet and fill them with his creations, the perfect genetic machine. The illuminated human being. Nergal again began the process of harvesting humans. This time he could genetically ensure obedience removing the ability to be defiant. These beings were genetically engineered to provide Nergal with their loyalty to death.

Nergal would need to continue reproducing more advanced Seraphim. He would flood the planet's surface with his kind. The future of his kind dependent on his ability to focus with the time he had on future endeavors. The time for planning and preparing had arrived outside the spotlight of the Nephilim, who Nergal were confident operated in complete disarray and confusion at the moment. The tower they had built towards the heavens now obsolete with their Nibiru destroyed, inoperable, floating away. The Nephilim true nomads, trapped to their ships in the sky. The surface covered in their cities filled with their Titans and advanced greys enslaving the humans and people of Ares on the surface.

The rest of the planet was covered either in death by planetary chaos or the many beasts that stalked the surface genetically programmed to devour. Humanity would have to survive living face to face with the mutated giant lizards. He did not have to deal with this problem. They were his own species only slightly mutated and a bit crazy. Nergal knew for the time being they would seek to rebuild their culture within the planet, the surface was far too dangerous. The grays working in groups of ten pressing deeper into the massive ice sheets, lower into the surface of the planet to plan the future of humanity on the planet against dark forces and alien predators.

What would become of the universe of origin?

www.ingramcontent.com/pod-product-compliance
Lightning Source LLC
Chambersburg PA
CBHW071406170626
46811CB00003B/1278